PRAISE FOR
ROUNDABOUT OF DEATH

"Sparse and harrowing ... Readers will find this fragmented tale of war-torn Aleppo and its displaced intellectuals chilling and insightful."

—*PUBLISHERS WEEKLY*

"News reports and images have exposed the horrors of the Syrian crisis: millions of refugees, bombing and chemical weapons. But this powerful novel by Faysal Khartash makes the grim reality of survival through the fierce fighting in Aleppo truly comprehensible."

—*ITAMAR RABINOVICH,*
co-author of *Syrian Requiem: The Civil War and its Aftermath*

"Some books stand as monuments to wars from which they arise. This is one of those books."

—ELLIOT ACKERMAN,
author of *Green on Blue* and *Waiting for Eden*

"A masterful distillation of one of the great tragedies of the twenty-first century, as stripped of artifice and sentimentality as it is undergirded with insight and empathy. *Roundabout of Death* is essential reading."

—DAN MAYLAND,
author of *The Doctor of Aleppo*

"A brilliant, kaleidoscopic and claustrophobic portrayal of the Syrian civil war. Khartash's spare prose eloquently conveys horrors that require no rhetorical elevation. This is a fine book that deserves a wide readership, both on its own merits and because the Syrian disaster is by no means over."

—JONATHAN SPYER,
author of *Days of the Fall: A Reporter's Journey in the Syria and Iraq Wars*

"Tells the incredible story of how the city of Aleppo has been reduced to piles of rubble and blood-soaked dirt in the wake of a celebrated history, its once proud identity now lost in the shadows."

—*AL-BAYAN* (Dubai)

"[Faysal Khartash] has always written imaginatively about the character of Aleppo, especially those relegated to the margins, the deep trenches, revealing the city's subterranean worlds. He intimately chronicles Aleppo's alleyways and secret corners, which is why most of his novels have faced state censorship."

—*AL-AKHBAR* (Beirut)

ROUNDABOUT

OF

DEATH

FAYSAL
KHARTASH

TRANSLATED FROM THE ARABIC
BY MAX WEISS

NEW VESSEL PRESS
NEW YORK

New Vessel Press

www.newvesselpress.com

First published in Arabic as *Dawwār al-mawt mā bayna Ḥalab wa-l -Raqqa*
Copyright © 2017 Faysal Khartash
Translation copyright © 2021 Max Weiss

Library of Congress Cataloging-in-Publication Data
Khartash, Faysal
[Dawwār al-mawt mā bayna Ḥalab wa-l-Raqqa, English]
Roundabout of Death/Faysal Khartash; translation by Max Weiss
p. cm.
ISBN 978-1-939931-92-4
Library of Congress Control Number 2020946573
I. Syria—Fiction

ROUNDABOUT OF DEATH

DEATH AND BOREDOM IN ALEPPO

The protagonist of *Roundabout of Death*, Faysal Khartash's searing 2017 novel set in wartime Aleppo, is a schoolteacher named Jumaa. Unemployed except for serving as the reader's guide through a hellish warscape, he has a harrowing tale to tell. Jumaa bears witness to the brutal series of sieges and counterattacks known as the Battle of Aleppo (2012–2016) that pulverized the northern Syrian metropolis after forces loyal to President Bashar al-Assad assaulted eastern sections of the city from both the air and the ground.

A few strange moments occur in the heat of the conflict. When Jumaa hallucinates about the appearance of tiny bumps—vaguely resembling horns—on his forehead, he perceives them as literal manifestations of his own sexual arousal and frustration. Jumaa's confusion here is precipitated not only by his own sense of impotence, but also by an accompanying and widely shared sentiment of shame.

This minor plot point gestures toward something profound at work in this short, trenchant novel, namely the rampant and, one might say, subcutaneous feeling of anomie and uncertainty that characterizes war-torn Aleppo. Let us call Jumaa's uncanny experience war phrenology: the somatic experience of wartime pathology that results in an impaired ability to comprehend the present as well as a persistent dread of an unpredictable future.

Syrians began to protest the Assad regime's corruption and unaccountability in 2010 and 2011 across small- to medium-sized cities all over the country, with sporadic demonstrations also erupting in the capital, Damascus. It wasn't clear during those initial phases whether these actions would congeal into a national movement capable of spreading through larger cities such as Homs and Hama. Most unforeseeable of all was Aleppo, whose large Armenian, Kurdish, Turkmen, and Turkish-speaking communities lend it the greatest religious and ethnic diversity of any Syrian municipality. Academics, policymakers, and the general public struggled to divine if and when this commercial capital of the country, a legendary city with striking cultural vibrancy and an outsize significance in the national mythology, might also be drawn into "the events" subsuming Syria as a whole. As the Syrian revolution gradually devolved into a chaotic, gruesome, and internationally fueled conflict, the war arrived in Aleppo with fury in the summer of 2012.

In the years that followed, the once-proud city accorded—albeit in vain—the protected status of a UNESCO World Heritage Site for its wealth of ancient monuments would be subjected to some of the fiercest, bloodiest, and most costly battles of the Syrian civil war. Iconic "barrel bombs" were dropped on Aleppo by regime aircraft, chemical weapons were unleashed on many districts, Russian military and material support conspicuously arrived to shore up regime forces, Lebanese Hezbollah fighters were marshaled into action, and militia outfits from the Kurdish and Armenian communities were drawn into urban guerilla warfare. This macabre symphony was performed in relation to and alongside the ongoing kinetic struggle between the Syrian regime's armed forces and opposition elements such as the Free Syrian Army, Jabhat al-Nusra, Ahrar al-Sham, and others.

The summer of 2016 was ruinous for Aleppo, leaving it reeling from the physical, economic, and human toll of nearly five years of calamitous combat. Now the regime launched a major new offensive against rebel-held areas, effectively strangling Aleppo by cutting it in half, opening the possibility of food shortages and total social collapse. There were estimates of just over 200,000 civilians and some 8,000 fighters left, compared with a population of more than two million before fighting broke out in 2012. Tens of thousands fled their city when, during the second half of that year, over 3,500 civilians were killed in shelling and airstrikes as the regime unleashed all weapons at its disposal—including illegal chemical weapons and improvised barrel bombs—ostensibly to root out "terrorists," but also destroying private homes, public spaces, and medical facilities in the process. This is the savage world from which Faysal Khartash's *Roundabout of Death* arose.

Khartash was born in Aleppo in 1952, part of a generation of disillusioned Syrian writers who were relatively isolated from the rest of their country and little-known outside of Syria. These Aleppan intellectuals nevertheless continued to live, write, and work, languishing away for many of their days in dingy, smoke-filled cafes, bars, and restaurants, under the alternatively lazy and watchful eye of state censorship. Most of Khartash's novels—including *Mūjaz Tārīkh al-Bāshā al-Ṣaghīr* (A Short History of the Little Pasha) (1991), *Khān al-Zaytūn* (The Olive Caravanserai) (1995), *Maqhā al-Majānīn* (The Lunatics' Cafe) (1995), *Ḥammām al-Niswān* (The Women's Bath) (1999), and *Maqhā al-Qasr* (Palace Cafe) (2004)—are set in the distinctive urban spaces of twentieth-century Aleppo: coffeehouses, public baths, and covered markets. His 1992 novel *Turāb al-Ghurabā'* (*Land of Strangers*), a fictionalized account of the life and times of the Ottoman-Aleppan intellectual and politician 'Abd al-Raḥmān al-Kawākibī, received the Naguib Mahfouz Prize for Arabic Literature and was adapted into a film by Syrian director Samir Zikra that was released in 1998. Khartash's 2018 novel *Ahl al-Hawā* (Lovers) was honored with the Tayeb Salih Prize for Novelistic Creativity.

Roundabout of Death is his first—but hopefully not last—novel to be published in English. As described above, life in general has already been violently disrupted across the divided city of Aleppo when the novel begins. Jumaa's attempts to maintain a modicum of regularity in his daily habits while also attending to the needs of his aging mother who lives across town provide the context within which the reader encounters a city and a country in seemingly unending conflict and crisis. The narrative voice erratically swerves from first-person limited perspective to third-person omniscient and back again. Perhaps more important than the polyphony of narrative perspective, though, is the complicated relationship Jumaa has to space, in personal and emotional terms, as well as to concrete, physical places in particular.

Along with a cohort of crusty intellectuals and unemployed middle-class men, Jumaa frequents smoke-filled cafes around the iconic Saadallah al-Jabiri Square in downtown Aleppo, not far from the university, a neighborhood that is now overtaken by displaced people, working prostitutes, and hordes of conscript soldiers and their commanding officers. From his coffee-shop perch overlooking the square, Jumaa is simultaneously witness to and (if only by the reader) witnessed in the never-ending calamity and deepening malaise. Like other literary narratives of wartime, therefore, *Roundabout of Death* is far from a romantic action story. On the contrary, ennui has set in for Jumaa and his companions. "Typically, there aren't too many of us," Jumaa notes, "ten people or so, give or take, including a doctor, a lawyer, and an unemployed teacher. Some are retired, some own their own businesses, some of us have lost our children and some are just waiting for no reason at all."

It would seem that the entire city of Aleppo—except for the hundreds of irregular fighters and thousands of soldiers in the midst of a punishing military conflict—is waiting for some semblance of normalcy to return.

Jumaa feels the absence of normal life most poignantly perhaps in his inability to regularly and easily check in on his mother, who lives on the other side of town, and much of the novel recounts the monotonous but impossibly circuitous route he must take—on foot, by bus, in private cars—to make the otherwise simple journey from the western part of the city to the east. The titular "death roundabout" is most likely a reference to the fearsome Karaj al-Hajez crossing point between the eastern and western sides of the city or another checkpoint much like it. Heading east, one can continue on to the city of Raqqa, one-time capital of the Islamic State of Iraq and Syria (ISIS). The original Arabic title of the novel translates literally to *The Roundabout of Death Between Aleppo and Raqqa*, and the physical obstacle and symbolic danger of that location are key to the physical and emotional geography of the text. But there are other locations in Jumaa's personal map of the city—Saadallah al-Jabiri Square first and foremost—in which he and his companions encounter an altogether different, though no less punishing, crossing: the intersection of boredom and uncertainty. Without understating the scale of physical destruction and human devastation in these times, it bears remembering that the individual and communal experiences of life in wartime are just as often felt in banal moments and quotidian routines.

By the middle of December 2016, Aleppo had been decisively flattened, at least hundreds of thousands of people had been internally displaced, many more had become refugees, and the regime claimed to have won a major military victory, one that may prove to have been Pyrrhic, although the local and national consequences of the Battle of Aleppo remain uncertain. Whatever the case, it is a cruel irony of history that the jaw-dropping and awe-inspiring city of Aleppo now seems to be inscribed in global consciousness at the moment of its annihilation. A comparable phenomenon—albeit less dramatic in terms of human costs—is also at work in the literary and cultural spheres, as writers such as Nihad Sirees, Khaled Khalifa, and now Faysal Khartash achieve a level of international attention unprecedented for Syrian writers, affirming the intellectual vitality of Aleppo even as the city confronts chilling and lethal realities.

Roundabout of Death can be read as a monumental testament to the power of literature as a means of documenting wartime atrocities, but one should not neglect to appreciate how such a literary text can also more modestly capture moments of psychological vulnerability, physical danger, and geographical remapping. Such moments have been experienced in diverse and contradictory ways by the people of Aleppo, both those who stayed and those who left. In light of such a literary achievement, moreover, there is good reason to retain some measure of hope. The dynamism and mordant wit of Aleppo's poets, intellectuals, and writers may well prove capable of transcending the tragedy of the present moment. Their celebration of the lives and history of Aleppo heralds, however hesitantly and unsurely, the city's unwritten and, one can only hope, happier future.

—Max Weiss

SAADALLAH AL-JABIRI SQUARE, ALEPPO

August 25, 2012
5:20 a.m.

I woke up at that time on the dot. The electricity had been cut. When I looked at the school wall directly across from me, I could see that the lights had gone out, replaced by a gloomy darkness. Every night the school became a beacon, and this window in particular shone until morning. It was as if the multitude had forgotten about the switch that could turn those neon lights that burned my eyes on as well as off.

My name is Jumaa Abd al-Jaleel. How I got my name is one of the simplest things in the world. That's just what my parents called me because of the day I was born, Friday, *Jumaa*. Though my mother and father had toyed with a few different names, this one won out in the end, and would remain attached to me throughout my life, perhaps even for a few years beyond that.

Abd al-Jaleel is my family name; I have no idea where it comes from. Never had much interest in looking into the matter, to be quite honest.

Jumaa Abd al-Jaleel snored abruptly and then woke up. The electricity hadn't been restored yet. There were so many things he had to do but he didn't get up . . . he waited for the electricity to come back on first.

You might ask, why did I use the word "multitude" in quoting what Jumaa had written?—"It was as if the multitude had forgotten . . . etc." Yes, my good people, there had been a multitude in the classroom for juniors at the high school until they'd moved all the chairs out and washed the floor, removed the remaining pieces of furniture and then spread mattresses all over the place. Throughout the day they would lie down whenever they got tired of talking with one another or walking around in circles, whether alone or in groups. At night they would lie down to take their rest but sleep with one eye open, afraid of death or even worse things to come.

The fighter jet starts to circle through the sky, soaring up and then swooping down, as if the pilot suddenly has something to take care of. What could cause him to zoom around like that up there, clearing away the pigeons, the sparrows, the doves, everything that flies? Was it all to free up the airspace for himself so that he could then just disappear? And where did he go anyhow? I have no idea. As he swoops down toward the ground, the pilot might declare, "The word 'bombs' is the most adequate to describe these objects that weigh precisely five hundred kilograms, something that explodes and destroys, that can relocate an entire building or a market, that can blow a hole in the middle of the street, causing the sewers and the water mains to flood, and lots of other things, too, of course." The pilot might also decide to jettison something off to the side that razes houses or shops or mosques, and whoever is left alive will simply have to wait for the next round of shelling, a role created for them . . . until the pilot completes his mission and returns safely back to base, washes his hands, runs off to scarf down his meal and head to sleep because it's well past his bedtime.

My head had always been round, but now it appeared to have become egg-shaped. At least that's the way it seemed as I looked at myself in the bathroom mirror; all of a sudden it was elongated, and it seemed as if there were two tiny bumps bulging out in arousal, making me look like some kind of sexual deviant, so I quickly smoothed down my hair to cover them. There might have been something wrong with the mirror, or maybe something wrong with me. I tried to call my friends at the cafe, but nobody picked up—why wouldn't anyone answer the phone? Probably because the electricity was cut, as you all know well, and the gas had run out a long time ago, it could have been a month, possibly more, I'm not sure. Well, why don't I just walk over to the cafe, I thought to myself. Even though the way there was littered with danger, I got ready to walk over anyway.

My cafe is located in Saadallah al-Jabiri Square, smack in the middle of the city, a secure area because it's under regime control. On the way there you pass by security headquarters, the university, and the mayor's mansion, all of which make the trip pretty complicated. I could add to that list the drones that target residents with wave after wave of bombs, although to be honest those drones and their weapons have never really gotten near me, and the sounds of the explosions don't really bother me too much because I know where they're coming from; they now seem to possess their own temporality as the explosions ring in our ears, turning sleep into a perpetual wish. The important thing in all of this is that I managed to put on my clothes and smooth down my hair, concealing the two small lumps I still believed I could see jutting from my forehead, before leaving the house.

On the way to the cafe there are a few burned-out houses—not a lot, but signs of destruction are everywhere. This can't be our street, no way: missile shells, tanks, a torched bus, which I think must belong to the regime, tons of tree branches, stones, and chimney remains, the sound of gunfire as militiamen open fire on one another. Some of them are with the regime, others aren't. A driver speeds forward and asks, "Any casualties?" Several voices answer, including my own, "Everyone's fine." He continues rushing ahead, a snorting guffaw spilling out of his mouth.

When I finally made it to our cafe, Joha's Club, I toddled inside. It's located in the same square as the business hotel, which is off to the right if you're sitting in the upper level, and the Officers' Club which is to the left. Directly across is the post office, and right next to that is a store where people who feel like buying things can go and buy things. In the middle of the square there is a statue by Abd al-Rahman Mowakket, the sculptor who sacrificed a good deal of his younger years to create a martyrs' monument that people could stand in front of breathlessly, snapping photos just to prove they were once in Aleppo.

Yesterday a missile screamed across the facade of the business hotel, at least that's how it seemed to me, and all of a sudden scores of soldiers from the Republican Guard sprinted out of the hotel and the Officers' Club so they could fan out in front, armed to the teeth, everyone in position, their fingers poised to pull the trigger. But the missile just sailed right past, nothing happened, and the soldiers from the Republican Guard relaxed their fingers, picked up their weapons, and went back inside the hotel. I didn't notice any soldiers going inside the Officers' Club.

This cafe—our cafe—is distinguished by its ancient Oriental atmosphere, at least that's the way it had been constructed, the owner flaked off every last bit of stone and painted the wood, furnished the place with lanterns and decorated the tables with cloths the same color as bathhouse towels. He put up a portrait of the trickster character of Joha along with some information about his biography and his exploits, crowned with a sign that read "Joha's Club, A Place for Everyone." Some of those people appear in a flash, down their coffee and then leave, while others never stop gazing out the window expectantly, because she just might show up. That's me, the one who's been waiting seven years for a woman who still hasn't come, the one who sips at his coffee and mentally records the thoughts rattling around in his mind, and even though he always carries his notebook with him, he always seems to forget that it's right there in his back pocket, and he always leaves his pen at home so there aren't any records or journal entries other than those he keeps stored in his head.

At the back of the cafe, which is to say, in the corner, sits the *Shabbih*, the Henchman, who takes his name from the Arabic word for ghost, which is also the nickname of a specific car that the *shabbiha* were known to drive in the eighties, racing around at top speed, transporting smuggled goods like cigarettes, electrical supplies, and other contraband. But this guy is a shabbih manqué: he has piled on top of his wooden cart assorted lighters and playing cards. At the other end of the cafe there's another shabbih who has spent his entire life hawking illicit tobacco, and when he had kids he stationed them by his side so they could learn the family business.

But how did I ever find out that these men were shabbiha? There's a story here I'd like to share with you, if you have the patience to hear me out.

Some days I get to the cafe at 11:30 a.m. and take a seat at a table, the waiter brings me a cup of instant coffee, a bit of sugar in a small bowl, two glasses of water in the summer, one in the winter, and I put a heaping amount of sugar into the cup and start to stir. I don't sip the coffee while it's hot, but wait until it has cooled off, at which point I'll drink it down in several gulps: I don't swallow it in one go like a camel.

One of those days there was an explosion in one of the tents scattered in the square. I think there had been seven tents, which were then winnowed down to five. They belonged largely to recently formed political parties, except for one that had been founded a long time ago, the Progressive Party, I think it's called. Some of them were there so they could write things in blood, which is to say they would spell out letters as large as several meters long scrawled in blood.

The important thing, my good people, is that the tents that had been scattered throughout the square were torn down and there were only two left standing. The shabbiha come and go around there day and night. One of those security goons who would pass by over there was very fat, and he'd just sit there humming to himself, at some point sauntering inside the business hotel, apparently to use the toilet. Customers in the hotel cafe started hurrying outside, one by one, holding their noses, until the entire place was cleared out and there was nobody left except for the employees, who were pressing handkerchiefs up against their noses. They had been there since early in the morning, before the fat guy ever went to use the bathroom, but the handkerchiefs ceased to provide enough protection, and everyone ended up outside, leaving the empty cafe to the fat man, who could now hum to his heart's content.

The employees and the staff who had been expecting the arrival of the fat man for an hour waited more than another hour for him to come back out, let's call it two hours all told. Some of them decided to take their lunch breaks and just up and left. And in light of the fact that there weren't that many customers around because of everything going on in the country, because of the artillery fire coming from all sides, they decided to shut down the business hotel. That was before the security forces even discovered the strategic significance of this place in relation to the square, at which point they quickly stocked the area with soldiers and snipers, stationing all of them in a room that directly overlooks the square as well as the streets branching off from it.

The fat man was thoroughly unaffected by all this. When they slammed shut the doors of the business hotel in his face, he casually wandered over to another cafe next door. Our cafe had nothing to do with the whole thing, thank God, because ours is located off to the left and twenty steps up off the ground—otherwise the fat man might have found it, which is to say that this guy isn't capable of climbing up to our bathrooms, or we would have been made a laughingstock—and where were we ever going to get another cafe like this one?

Like I said, there was an explosion in the square, possibly inside one of the tents, the shabbiha tent—well, all of the tents belonged to the shabbiha. A man was thrown out of the tent, tearing apart the canvas as another came out carrying someone on his back, and they were thrown onto the green grass; then the shell of another man came through the door of the tent, followed by another, then another. Then it was time for the shabbiha who were stationed outside of the square, and they came running in droves, each one of them toting a Russian-made 7.62mm rifle and shouting at everyone—Clear the streets, you dogs!—and other things I'm too ashamed to write down.

They stopped every taxi they could find and filled them with the wounded, rushing them off to the hospital. As I sat there, I was able to watch everything that was happening through the window, as the shabbiha ran through the streets for a long time, hollering, waving their arms, hoisting up their weapons. Other armed factions responded by shooting into the air from far off in the distance. Then someone rolled up in a Mercedes to write a report about what had taken place, and a policeman handed them a satellite phone, telling them that he needed to go to the Party Bureau, asking them to hold on to the phone until he returned, just for a little while, and no more than half an hour had passed before the device blew up and wounded a number of people. The investigation was complete, and the news was broadcast on Syrian television.

But that isn't the whole story. Those young men were in good spirits, they were having a good time, tossing around a grenade, this one throwing it here, another one hurling it over there. But it was when one of those geniuses decided to pull the pin and chuck it at his comrade, who tossed it right back, that there was an explosion, and then everything else that happened happened.

Miss Beauties was her stage persona, she never told anyone her real name. She used to sneak into the square from the side of the hotel cafe. I saw her with my own two eyes, the same ones the worms will feed on one day. The shabbih who sells lighters also saw her and warned her to get away, but she didn't pay any attention to what he said, simply placing her finger over her mouth and shaking her head side to side, shimmying part of her body, just the upper half, asking him to allow her to pass. He refused sternly, telling her, "Get the hell out of here, you whore, this isn't your time."

What matters, though, my good people, is that eventually he did let her pass, and Miss Beauties rushed right past and took shelter in the corner, with a *tabac* proprietor who was no longer in his kiosk because he too was a shabbih, now toting a Russian-made machine gun and standing in the middle of the street, holding up his hand to stop people and cars and motorcycles from passing, hurling curses at them, seemingly without limits.

It turns out that Miss Beauties was in need of a cigarette, so she stopped there, unaffected by what was going on all around her, gazing at the *tabac*, casing the joint, then thrusting out her hand to swipe a pack of Kents, and when she was certain that the coast was clear, she shoved it in her pants pocket, and started to walk away, but just then the shabbih who owned the place spotted her, shot some rounds into the air and shouted at her—"I see you, you whore!"—but she just smiled at him and shuffled off.

"You're gonna have to pay for those!"

But because he was tied up at the moment blocking traffic, and had forced everyone up against the walls with his rifle, he had no choice but to let her get away, and she raced over to the courtyard of the hotel cafe, sat down on the pavement, and unwrapped the pack of cigarettes. She took one out and lit it up, her smile seeming to fill up the entire expanse of existence, sucking down a drag and then exhaling the smoke.

Her entire body seemed to unwind, and in that moment it occurred to her that the entire space was being filled with the sound of her own voice, as she took another drag, remembered her village and all the people who had fled, her husband who used to beat her, she remembered all that and spat loudly on the asphalt, then got up and staggered forward.

Miss Beauties was the name by which the shabbih called her when he first noticed her. He had been popping pills all day long, and had drunk a few bottles of strong beer, until he was so drunk a rooster looked like a donkey to him, the pills caused him to see this world all beautiful, sunny, and rose-colored, and he fell into a deep sleep in which the world would never change. But when he awoke, he could feel that the pills were wearing off, so he quickly swallowed another one. His body was starting to relax once again when he noticed her at the entrance to the tent smirking at him in all her glory, wearing pants and a blouse unbuttoned down to her chest, her bronze hair, and spittle shot toward her as he shouted, "Where have you been, Miss Beauties?"

"I'm right here," she replied.

As she collapsed into his lap, he kissed her, then got up to shut the door, unfurl the tent canvas and switch off the light. Only faint streetlight leaked into the room. In rhythm with the sound of the explosions their bleating moans of pleasure started to swell.

The shabbih was named Jassim, but he slurred a bit when he spoke, pronouncing it as Qassim; he had made a living selling smuggled tobacco ever since he was a little boy, that is to say, from the age of seven or eight. His brother would deliver the haul of tobacco and then cower behind him; if they ever encountered the authorities his older brother would disappear, leaving him in tears, which would typically cause the officials to do no more than seize a few cartons of tobacco and then let him go.

When he got older he was sent off to prison, graduated from that institution with the rank of informant, and no longer smuggled tobacco, darting from cafe to cafe instead, anyone who needed the stuff coming to a kiosk he set up selling many varieties. He'd sit behind the counter, conducting his business, and when the authorities came around, he'd hand them eight thousand lira so they would continue on their merry way. The auxiliary police patrol would also come by to take their cut and then disappear. He never threw his weight around to intimidate anybody, and the truth of the matter is that he was quite well-mannered.

But events got the better of him, and soon he was stashing a machine gun under his counter, and anytime there was some kind of an incident in Saadallah al-Jabiri Square, we'd see him holding up his weapon and insulting everyone, preventing anybody from going anywhere.

Qassim—whose name had once been Jassim, before he started to slur—used to take pills, he was a pill-popper, his brother had gotten him hooked, it wasn't miscreant kids or those who spread rumors about him. For a long time he wouldn't partake because he saw what befell his brother whenever he got high. One time he went to the pharmacy and just asked for some pills straight out, and when the pharmacist refused he immediately threatened him with a knife, which was enough to persuade the pharmacist to hurriedly hand over what he wanted without taking any money.

His brother dropped the pill into a cup of tea, drank it down, and felt no pain. He became a king, giving out orders and always being obeyed. "Do this," he barked, and everyone would do it, and he would laugh at himself and all the people, and from that day forward he couldn't live without that feeling, until he got addicted to sticking a needle into his left arm and his right, and you'd always see him playing the sultan like that. From early in the morning he'd sit against the wall of the cafe, his movable counter replete with cigarettes of every make and color laid out in front of him until it was time for his afternoon fix, and he'd get up and carry his kiosk to the adjoining wall where he would lie down until nighttime, when exhaustion overcame him, and he would roll up his wares, fold the kiosk in on itself, and go off to sleep in the tent, scrounging whatever he could find to eat, and if he didn't find anything then he'd totter off for a bit and come back with two sandwiches from the falafel seller, voraciously wolfing them down, and then falling asleep . . . until she showed up to see him that night, and everything that happened happened.

Meanwhile Miss Beauties, who was all messed up that night, had gone to visit a couple of intellectuals who took turns having their way with her, fed her some bread and eggs, and then gave it to her a second time. A singer came over later and had a turn with her, then a washed-up actor from some television serial showed up and had his way with her, too. When everyone had had their turn, they kicked her out, and she was neither sad nor happy as she left, utter bewilderment written all over her face as she traipsed around the garden and then started singing out loud. When they heard her over at the security station, they ordered her to keep it down, and when she refused they conceded to let her keep singing on the condition that she not let them see her face, and so she walked off in the direction of Saadallah al-Jabiri Square.

The square was as quiet as marble, darkness enthroned all around: no movement, no sound except for her singing voice. Snipers' sights peered down from the rooftops, and when they heard her sorrow-soaked voice they were dumbstruck, wishing their two-hour shift was over so they could go get some sleep. Some of the men were moved to think of their wives, some remembered their brothers and sisters, others thought of their friends, the way they used to be when they were together, whether they were in a serious or a joking mood, or something else altogether. But in that moment most of them thought of their own mother, some of them teared up and marinated in those memories, as if she were right there with them, suspended in their imaginations, visible as if in front of their eyes.

When Miss Beauties cried out the flowers all around responded to her, along with the trees swaying in the park and the plants under the monument, and the breeze gliding over the water, and the leaves that started to turn all dewy with the first tidings of dusk, and the monument itself that had been solid until that very moment, and how the tears streamed down Abdel Rahman's face for a moment, and the cry erupted from Miss Beauties's mouth, as if she were breathing fire.

Before the intellectuals had their way with her and then sent her packing, a woman whose name I forget came into the city. She didn't know the first thing about what was going on. The army and the security forces had invaded her village that day. She fled to the left and her husband ran off to the right, and their two children Hassan and Naimah went to hide in the cave on their neighbor Bikro's property. She kept walking, the bombs falling all around her, until she reached the main road, where she saw convoys of tanks and armored cars. She was frightened and shivered, then turned back the way she had come. She took shelter under an olive tree, burying her head against her knees, remaining like that until nightfall, then she lifted her face to consider her situation. Day broke, slowly illuminating the night, at first she just laughed, laughed a second time, then frowned. She stood up tall, gazed into the pitch-black darkness, shielding her eyes with her hand, and swiveling her head. Unable to make out anything, she took a few confident steps until the road became clearer and she kept on walking until she made it to the city. She sat down in the middle of the street until an intellectual happened to find her, take pity on her, and take her home with him.

This particular intellectual had a deaf and blind mother who didn't have a clue about what was going on, especially the fact that he was having friends over every night. His mother went to sleep early and they would stay up late into the night, and when he kicked Miss Beauties out, they all got to work cleaning up the house, stripping the bed, and washing the sheets.

Miss Beauties—and this was all before that name had been affixed to her, mind you—used to walk through the streets and the squares, until what happened happened and she slept with that shabbih, who as soon as he had finished his business let his mind drift off until he fell asleep. Seeing as how there were two beds inside the tent, he lay down on the second one, and she picked up his pack of cigarettes and lit one. Pants were strewn underneath the bed, and she picked up her underwear and put them on, buttoned up her shirt. She finished the cigarette, started to remember everything that had happened to her, and gradually she too floated out of wakefulness amid thoughts of the peaceful village she had left behind, her husband and her children, but then she forgot about everything, forgot her husband and her children and her village, and the women who used to sit with her every night, forgot her own memory even, now could no longer remember what had happened to her or who had done what with her, until finally she fell asleep.

The intensity of the shelling didn't prevent this wounded dove from thinking about how much she loved her son, how willing she was to go starving in order to feed him. Here he is, her little chicken beside the window, squawking as he waits for his mother to arrive, his dilated eyes frantically staring out in all directions. Would he notice all of the military equipment that had been cleaned and then installed on the balconies of the business hotel, where all the snipers were stationed early in the morning before the sun came up and before the women came out to tell the men, "Here I am, I'm coming to see you"? They had all done their hair and prettied themselves up with makeup as soon as they awoke, which quickly electrified the city and all the people who had just woken up as well, each and every one of whom had to rely entirely on themselves to get up and go to work.

Here is that mother coming back home again, her little chicken pressing his beak against hers as she shoves specks of grain into his mouth, or any other morsels she could find. The two of them are refreshed: the little chicken hops on top of her and yanks the kernel out of her beak even as she shoves it into his. And here's a Rio car stopping in the middle of the square, alongside the Dushka, and three people creep up to search the vehicle. One of them opens the trunk, places a little chicken inside, no, it's not a bird, it's a human being, he has been plucked from the business hotel, his hands bound and his eyes covered with a blindfold, then they slam the trunk shut and the car speeds away.

Every day I sit right here, watching the square, Saadallah al-Jabiri Square. And, oh, how has it changed.

It was designed by one of our comrades in this form so that marches could easily be assembled, so that slogans could be chanted, so that students could gather here, all the way from first grade through their higher education. To that

I'd also have to add all the professors and teachers, all the doctors and every patient who seeks their counsel, all the party bosses, government officials, and security apparatchiks, men and women, all congregating together, all with their own paraphernalia, be those images or posters, all of which are distributed in the morning, and which they bring out with them in the evening. I carry something, comrade, and another comrade or two carries an image of the sacrificing Leader. Security officials of all stripes are spread throughout the square, along with all divisions of the police, and the Party membership in all of its glory, and members of the National Front at all levels, and that's how the demonstration becomes a million strong, even more, you might say.

Once, before the space was transformed into a square, there was a tramway that passed through here, a green and yellow one, and the business hotel was only two stories tall. Now there are six blocks, off to the right coming from Shukri al-Quwwatli Square, named after the first president of the republic, and from the left, here at the cafe, where I sit, in a landmarked property of the Islamic religious endowment.

Also off to the left there is Mosul Street, which runs into the Officers' Club, then a brothel, crawling with beautiful ladies from all over the world. There was an artist who used to hang out there, running his paintbrush all over the chairs. Outside of the brothel, toward the main street, there was the Republic Cinema, and next to that there was a falafel restaurant and another cafe that was open year round, and between those two places a Party branch with two guards always stationed outside, one to the right and one to the left, flanking the entrance, both very nice even though each of them sported a Russian-made rifle.

The Quwaik River runs right through the middle of the square that wasn't a square back in those days, Aleppo's river where we all used to swim over by the Turtle Bridge.

Back then someone came and built walls around the river. They laid down concrete and contained the water inside, turned the place into a public park, and then brought small boats to transport people.

Then a capitalist showed up, poured a cement carpet over the river, laid down a silk covering on top of that, and then shiny cobblestones that the masses could walk along as they praised the Leader.

A few Toyotas had arrived in the area carrying officials who were all wearing matching green uniforms and assorted sneakers. They fanned out across the square with Russian-made rifles, took several laps around, maybe five or more, I'm not sure exactly, didn't count, I guess, then they all started to advance toward the business hotel, and at that moment everyone inside came out into the street and started shouting, "Hey, hey, hey. . ." They had yellow bands wrapped around their arms, some had tied yellow cloths around their foreheads. The soldiers stood there, motionless, for half an hour, their guns at the ready. The officials in the Officers' Club came out to greet them, saying hello to some by shaking hands, some kissed one another, perhaps they already knew each other. Maybe those who were members of the shabbiha weren't supposed to be there long because they took off after making several laps around the place, which was filled with the sounds of kissing and shouting and Hey hey hey. . .

A Palestinian showed up, someone I had met recently. And Jamal, whom I have known for a long time, came around to tell me that my house had been bombed. We were all silent. Jamal is a little bit overweight, well, not just a little, you can think of him as being very fat. The Palestinian guy likes to call him Axis of Evil. He sat down at our table and lit up a long Marlboro Red. He took a sip of water and started to unload, telling us how he had just been at his house an hour ago when all five stories came crashing down, and because his house was like a garden, it absorbed the five floors in their entirety, crushing all the glass and the metal.

It was time for me to go home. But before I did, I passed by Bab Antakya and then Al-Saqatiyah to buy some meat as my wife had asked me to do.

I found my way over to the Hanging Gardens Gate, that's what we called it anyway. The cobblers were fixing up people's shoes while they waited. All along the southern wall, between the two gates—the Hanging Gardens Gate and Bab Antakya—the cobblers had either dug in or, if not dug in, they had rented out shops where they could repair shoes. And bring us a black market.

When you come out of that black market, you reach a small mosque, I don't know who built it, and I'm not going to try to find out. I see an airplane circling high up in the sky—the word circling is just long enough to communicate the experience—before it swoops down. It's a MiG-32, as far as I can tell, and now the plane is striking, launching its missiles. "Let's move, brother! Looks like this one could hit us." I'm convinced Seven Seas Square is the real target. *BOOOOOM*. The people all jump up and scatter in every direction, and just like that everyone's eyes shift down to stare at their hands. Apparently some text messages sent by young men who mill about in the markets and the areas controlled by the Free Syrian Army had gone through. The missiles hit their targets, and the pilot carried out another sortie with great skill, then a third, raining bombs on the residential homes before flying away.

After you turn past the mosque you come to the cobblers, where one after another of them will greet you and invite you into his shop to tout flats, half heels, high heels. During this time you'll find the guy frying up kibbeh in oil, splitting it in half on the grill and sprinkling fried red pepper pods alongside. People cram all around him, some eating and others waiting their turn to receive their wrap, still others holding their meal and waiting for their bottle of ayran yogurt drink even as he wipes the sweat from his brow and prays to God for strength.

And there's the beloved rooftop restaurant that serves kebab with spiced Aleppan pistachios. Inside there are Bedouins, people from nearby villages eating, furniture merchants: they all pay full price these days. When a shell comes crashing down, whether fired from a tank or a plane or even from field artillery, the people scatter and drive off in their Trela trucks or their Suzuki jeeps, loading them up with women and children and the elderly, driving around the city several times to drop people off. If they can find anyone who'll take them in, the drivers will let them out near the monument, where the men will wait with them for as long as two hours before they'll take them back. And here come people carrying foam bedding and sheets, spreading them out to cover half the street, stretching it out as far as they can. Some of them set up shop there, unfolding all the bedding and then starting to set up tents. "We've got a house now, my child, don't worry." They awaken at dawn, praying to God as they watch the sunrise, then shake their weary heads.

BAB ANTAKYA

Here we are, in front of Bab Antakya; heaps of massive stone have been piled on top of each other in order to form this gigantic entryway. I cross under this Byzantine gate, which not even the fiercest armies were ever able to breach, to arrive at the mosque. Turning back, throwing a second glance in that direction . . . I can no longer see it. I think somebody must have taken it away, convincing myself they are stealing history itself, before continuing on my way unfazed.

I walk ahead a bit to the Al-Shuaibiyah mosque, finding an armed guard stationed there, then another, then another until they add up to five. One is wearing a mask, he could be with the Free Syrian Army, I think to myself, and it turns out that, yes, they are all with the Free Syrian Army, I can tell because they aren't wearing standardized uniforms, they're just slumped back in chairs with their fingers resting on gun triggers.

The city has been divided into east and west by these same hands of the Free Syrian Army: the west and a sliver of the north are with the regime army, now engaged in a battle for neighborhoods here and there.

The regime security services have made use of the *Mardel*, a strike force comprised of Kurds trained and armed as part of the state's own paramilitaries and integrated into its cadres; they have also made use of the Armenian community, which allowed them to continue playing dominoes in the middle of the street without any worries. All that matters to them is that no rockets fall on their houses, which is also the case for the Christian community in general, whose leader claimed that they are not for the regime but for the stability of the country, which is to say, one foot in heaven and the other foot in hell. In other words, if this foot leans one way, they lean with it, and if the other goes the other way, they are bound to that one as well.

Professor Joubran is an accomplished painter who ships his canvases to Beirut, and from there they are sent all over the world. Not too long ago a car bomb exploded near his studio, setting it ablaze.

I happened to overhear Professor Joubran say all of this during a conversation he was having at the cafe. He added how distraught he was about everyone who got killed, whether they were police or anybody else. When he was finished speaking, I asked him why he didn't write up a report explaining what had happened to him and then submit it to the mayoralty.

"What makes you think I didn't?" he retorted. "I submitted a report to the alderman, and he transmitted it to the mayor."

"And what happened?"

"They sent me two hundred liters of diesel oil to keep warm."

A staggering silence settled over us, an indeterminate silence, more eloquent than anything that could have been said.

And here I now find myself slithering eastward through the marketplace. I encounter people from the countryside just outside the city who have come to buy goods or make deals without buying anything right away. Continuing toward the east I leave the souq behind me and come to the small plaza outside the Al-Faqqas bathhouse. Here, too, there are Free Syrian Army forces with Russian rifles in their hands scattered around the square. I totter onto Al-Qassab Street, breathing in the aroma of meat from outside the entrance, and as soon as I get inside I find fresh flesh hanging from metal hooks.

APOCALYPSE NOW

I think this is the title of a film I saw once, maybe it was by Pasolini or Fellini, something like that. It was 1:35 p.m. as I walked in the direction of my mother's house. I was administering a kind of self-care by sipping a cup of tea, sitting there with her on the patio, surrounded by five of my brother's children.

I entered the Al-Telal neighborhood, where only a few shops remained open, while the rest had been shut. There were some men walking here and there, and by the time I reached the old fire station I saw about twenty soldiers from the regime's army spread out all over the place, brandishing their weapons, blocking the Free Syrian Army from breaching the Aziziyeh neighborhood from another front. I didn't greet any of them because I was suddenly overcome with a shudder of panic, especially once they started to haphazardly open fire into the air.

My daughter called me on my cell phone to tell me, after saying hello and asking how I was, that I shouldn't go to her grandmother's house. But why? Because she had received a phone call from my mother insisting that I shouldn't come because the shelling and the gunfire were like a heavy downpour. All right, I told her, even though I kept walking, looking up at the sky after I heard the sound of a screeching jet plane, which plummeted, spinning toward the area behind my mother's house, where it dropped its payload. My mother's house is near the central square while I'm in the new part of Aleppo and, my God, just look at what a distance I still have to traverse.

I continued walking at a measured pace as I watched women who had taken off half their clothes or even more than that as they bought vegetables and meat. When I reached the bakery, women were lined up on the right and men were lined up on the left. These people cannot find enough bread to eat, in a country covered with wheat. Even now you find them mobbing the bakeries; here there were nearly fifty women off to the right and a hundred men on the left. I hadn't made it yet, though. There were still two blocks to go before I would make it to her.

"How did you get here?" she asked. "Didn't I tell your daughter that you shouldn't come?" "What's done is done," I said. "I'll make you some tea," she said. "Go right ahead," I told her.

As she got up, I looked over at the five children. Her preparation of the tea and bringing it out onto the patio is a beautiful ritual. In that moment I was enjoying this small pleasure that I kept buried deep down inside: the way she poured the tea, how the children lined up alongside her, the way she poured a splash of water into each cup to cool off the tea, how they would sit around her, so respectful and well-mannered, all with the tacit understanding that at any moment we might be confronted with a sudden airstrike that could pounce upon the neighborhood just behind us, and then hear horrifying sounds caused by those explosions.

She was sad, and I asked her why. She didn't respond, silently handing the children their cups. When I asked her a second time, it turned out that her stoicism had its limits, and she burst out crying, informing me that a sniper had shot Fatima.

"What?!" I asked.

"Yes, they shot your cousin Fatima," she repeated.

Couldn't they have found someone besides Fatima? She was poor and disheveled, we had all helped to raise her after her father passed away and her mother got remarried. My mother took the most responsibility in raising her, both her and her sister actually, until she grew up and married a poor man. She ended up having, I don't know, four or five daughters, I had met some of them, they were beautiful, blonde, their eyes were broad and green.

"How did this happen?"

"She left her house in Al-Arqoub after it was destroyed, caught between the Free Syrian Army and the regime forces, she fled and rented a place in the Maysaloun neighborhood, where she was standing with her husband when they shot her from the minaret."

The minaret of the Shaykh Abu Bakr mosque, where my mother used to say prayers and blessings for us. I distracted myself by sipping the tea when my mother fell silent. My brother's wife's voice called out to the children that they should go and get dressed. "The woman is going to leave," my mother told me, "she's going to get her family together and leave . . ."

"And go where?"

"To stay with her family, or to their workshop in Al-Sulaymaniyah, it's a Christian neighborhood that isn't in danger of being hit . . ."

"I'm going, too."

"They buried her at the cemetery today, I don't know which one . . ."

"The modern cemetery."

"They all went to bury her, your sisters, their husbands, they all went to bury her, poor thing, she died at the same age as her father."

I slunk back outside as feelings of disgust and mercy, misery and pity washed over me. As I walked into the street, a plane dipped in my direction, swooped down and dropped its bomb. I could hear the sound of an explosion, then another one and another. More explosions would come later.

COCK FIGHT

Here I am going inside our cafe, Joha's Club, where I find my regular seat unoccupied. Maybe today won't be like all the others. I hear the sound of a fighter jet in the sky, nothing else but the sound of explosions. The soldier posted at the corner of the business hotel has cordoned off the sidewalk with decrepit metal objects. He's watching over the street, perhaps he's singing now, no longer concerned with much of anything at all. He has laid down his rifle in front of him, between the telephone wire and the little mailbox, leaving an opening no more than ten centimeters wide. A GMC truck is parked right outside the front door, transporting a DShK and a PKS machine gun on its roof. I notice a phalanx of soldiers forcing people who are carrying bread down onto the pavement where cars normally fly by, but there are no vehicles going past right now. They have blocked off the road from up by the club, or even before the club, all the way from the gas station down here, all the way to the beginning of the Jumayliyah neighborhood.

I tried to call my mother. And here I am now trying a second and a third time but failing to get through. I find myself getting embroiled in a conversation with the crew, the regulars at the cafe, a conversation about what took place yesterday. We no longer give a damn about exactly what happened or where the bombing took place as much as we want to talk about where the clashes were. The conversation was still raging as I tried calling my mother, but the recorded message said, "The number you have dialed is unavailable..." Just then I got through, the phone was ringing in my ear, I couldn't believe it, and the ringing continued until she picked up.

"Who is it?" she asked.

"It's me, Jumaa, your son," I said. "How are you? The line's been busy, everybody must have wanted to check in on you, see how you're doing."

She burst into tears, bawling as she told me, "My house is ruined, it's been totally destroyed. What am I supposed to do now? I'm just sitting here at your sister's."

She continued weeping. It had been a long time since I had heard her cry like this, or maybe I had never heard her cry at all until today. She mumbled some words I couldn't make out, concluding with, "May God give you endurance."

"Stay away from there," she said. "They're bombing everywhere and the fighting is as fierce as a cock fight, gunfire like a storm from hell ... don't come over here, son. I left the house and just ran away. I beg of you, don't come here."

Her voice faltered and the sound of her weeping echoed in my ear. I was overcome with sorrow and bitterness. I didn't say a word, kept silent, distracted myself by observing the pine tree in the public park. The treetop was so tall, it seemed boastful and proud, it could have been the first tree ever planted in this park.

Soldiers and other security officers were coming and going, spitting and snorting all the way.

The Palestinian shared that his son had begun experiencing extreme phobias the day before. He had gone to consult the doctor about this, but the doctor replied that it wasn't anything serious. The Palestinian said that his son would start convulsing whenever he heard the sound of a missile, and after the seizure stopped, he would lie down in his father's lap and start crying. The doctor said this was all very normal.

"How old is the boy?"

"Sixteen," the Palestinian answered.

"It's normal and happens in the best of families," the doctor reassured him.

Muhammad D joined the conversation. When asked how things were with him, he turned toward me and replied animatedly, "Oh geez, I'm not a real man, I guess: I live in Souq Al-Hal." He doesn't live in Souq al-Hal, though, he lives in an adjacent neighborhood, where all kinds of missiles have fallen. He turned to the Palestinian guy to ask if the word "missiles" was the correct nomenclature, whether he should use that term or "projectiles" instead . . . the Palestinian told him to carry on without offering an opinion on which word was more appropriate.

"In the square opposite Bab Antakya," Muhammad D continued, "there are sounds that come together in the night, these coming from the Al-Kalasa neighborhood, those from Bab al-Jinan, and others coming from Bab Antakya."

"Muhammad D can sit on the balcony and watch the battles while he smokes," the doctor told him.

"No, man," I said. "You need to get inside the house. When there's an incident or a battle happening, find a protected room and sit in there."

"But which one is actually protected?" Muhammad D asked. "The only room that doesn't look out on the street, the one you would call protected, also has a window, and it's well within the range of the security forces, I mean, as soon as I stick my head out they could shoot me right away. Just let God sort it out, man."

I needed to call my mother. I'm so very nervous about her and about the house. Something was eating at me, a lump in my throat was strangling me, clogging my respiratory system. "I have to go," said a man at the table that looks out on the square. "Why are they all gathered out there?" We stood up and stared at the scene. They were filming and conducting interviews with some passersby who said there was nothing happening in the square, that everything was peaches and cream, and may God punish the armed gangs who had dragged the country down into such violence.

THE SCHOOL OPENS ITS DOORS

The school is opening its doors today, the students are waking up early, slinging on their backpacks, and heading over. That's all in the past, though, when Jumaa the Teacher himself was going to school for the first day, and he was always a little bit late, to the point that his students would be lined up waiting to get into their classes. Here they are assembling together, missing out on first period, and so they start shouting out their names—So-and-So, grade one, Such-and-Such, grade one, and so on and so forth until they have eaten into second period, by which point Jumaa the Teacher will have finally shown up.

He lumbers into class, dragging his feet, the sun still struggling to rise in the sky. The early days of September are merciless, the heat scorches people's heads. Jumaa the Teacher begins by asking students their names, which schools they come from, until third period is over, the bell rings, and the students all start to shout, "Hey! Hey!" At this point Jumaa the Teacher likes to stroll down to the teacher's lounge so he can say hello to his friends and veteran colleagues, while freshman teachers slump into chairs by the entrance. Once the entire staff is present, the headmaster introduces everyone, or invites them to introduce themselves.

But today nothing of the sort is going to happen, because classes have been suspended—and why is that? Because some schools are with the Free Syrian Army now and some are with the regime, some have been converted into storehouses for airplane parts and projectiles, while others are secure, although some of those are occupied by internally displaced people, and still others have been destroyed by tank blasts and artillery, and so forth and so on.

We would visit the schools that appeared on the agenda, write down all the names and then sign the form, sit down for a spell before asking the following question: "Is there anything else, Miss?" Normally she would reply, "No, there's nothing else," and then she would declare, "We're glad to see that everything's fine."

Jumaa the Teacher chose a school near the technical college because it was close by. He took a shared taxi and got out in front, wrote down his name, gave his signature, and went to the cafe. Jumaa the Teacher had selected that school in particular because it was a high school, whereas the only schools near his house were a primary and a middle school.

Jumaa the Teacher had only ever taught in a high school that was located in the Sulayman al-Halabi neighborhood, where he taught the Arabic language. He would walk into class, read texts and teach grammar: the subject is always in the nominative case, whether substantive or undefined. And the object is cased similarly in the accusative, either substantive or undefined, dragging the genitive along with it, again whether substantive or undefined. Jumaa knows the prepositions, the particles of exception, and various forms of clarification and conditionality. You might say he knows all the ins and outs of Arabic grammar because he has spent such a long time teaching it, having now reached the brink of retirement.

He constantly quarrels with the headmaster about mistakes made at the school. He never shuts up, which may be why nobody can stand him except for this little crew that sits with him at the cafe. When they get into discussions about politics, he'll throw himself into it with abandon, offering an opinion that leaves people scratching their heads, even if they eventually absorb what he's saying without ever accepting his perspective. He always blurts out muddled views, this despite the fact that he watches TV every day, paying close attention to what they are saying, listens to the Arabic-language broadcast on Al-Jazeera, passionately following what is happening. Jumaa the Teacher is stern in his classes, to the benefit of his students to be sure, and he begins every class with, "Take out your books, anyone who doesn't have their book?" He gestures toward the door, and some students will leave, huddling by the door until class is finished, at which point he goes to ask a student representative to escort them to the headmaster. Since the headmaster is tired of this broken record, he instructs the representative to take them back to the disciplinarian, and so they walk back behind him, and when Jumaa opens the door for them, with only eight or nine students remaining in class with their books, only then will he start his lesson.

So much for the students in third grade science and literature. There are just two elective sections remaining, in which Jumaa the Teacher can offer either reading or composition.

Now he's off to the cafe, surveying Saadallah al-Jabiri Square, noticing but trying to ignore two Dushka machine guns, sensing without acknowledging the armed soldiers, and then reaching his usual spot where he can relax for a bit before the political talk gets going.

Once the political conversation starts, there is nobody more disagreeable: on one occasion he'll side with the Free Syrian Army, on another with the regime, occasionally he'll be opposed to the use of violence or the emergence of the Free Syrian Army, while at other times he'll argue against both the opposition in exile and that inside the country, claiming that the opposition is responsible for all this destruction, that if it weren't for them there wouldn't have been any of this killing and ruination in the first place. And when someone disagrees, he'll fiercely defend his idea, fighting to support his position, letting no one else say a word, but without ever shouting them down.

And so everyone grew extremely familiar with his debate style; they'd follow along as he expressed his opinion, hearing him out, but never reveal their own thoughts on the subject. As for why Jumaa the Teacher behaved that way, there's a story.

TWO LITTLE BUMPS
ON TOP OF MY HEAD

I stood in front of the mirror straightening my hair. The comb hurt as soon as I pressed it against my scalp. I pulled my hair aside and suddenly felt those strange bumps of arousal poking through once again. I styled my hair in a way that kept them hidden, so that nobody would be able to see them. I got dressed in a hurry because I needed to go inspect my mother's place. There was no longer any reply on her cell phone, and I needed to see for myself what had happened.

Schools hadn't opened their doors to students that day either, you might say they had opened one door and one door only, that of the administration, so that teachers could go inside, while all of the classrooms and other spaces—including the security station, the library, and the staff offices—had been turned into shelters for displaced people.

The refugees removed all the chairs from the classrooms and other spaces so that they could put down foam bedding, string up what passed for blinds over the windows, and pound nails into the walls so that they could hang up their belongings. The gas was communal, more or less, and when the canister ran out and there was no longer any fuel to be found, someone would go buy some or else they would find electric heaters. They began telling each other stories about the destruction and devastation that had befallen their homes. Then, bit by bit, the conversation would turn toward less serious matters, because it wasn't possible to talk about such things forever.

One of them asked why they didn't build something that would allow them, meaning the displaced people, to be able to feed themselves. The people sleeping in the schools awoke to the sound of that person's voice shouting, "Oh my God!" Someone had brought a watermelon from the farmers' market and laid it out in front of everyone. Another person brought grapes and so forth and so on, until the entire scene was filled out, and you could see fires and smoke, eggplants of all varieties, tomatoes, zucchini, and pumpkins. Someone made coffee and tea while someone else fried falafel and boiled eggs; another person made sandwiches with cured meats, tomatoes, and pickles for everyone to eat. In short the people started producing things to eat, including pita bread and other kinds. You would soon start to find everything from electronic goods to plumbing equipment; you might say an entire market had sprung up, including vendors of vegetables, bags of potato chips, all kinds of oil, country-style, animal-fat and industrial ghee, as well as chamomile and *mulukhiyah* leaves. I'm telling you, it would make your head spin.

Jumaa the Teacher, who was deeply involved in the whole thing, dropped by the school in order to sign in, then sat down with the administration.

"Everything all right, brother?" the female principal asked him.

"Aren't you going to sign this?" he asked her in turn.

"I wasn't aware you were a teacher here."

Jumaa the Teacher signed in and then walked away in a huff.

It was a calm morning, everything on our west side of the city was chaotic, cars were driving the wrong way on the roads. If people were driving the wrong way, though, that was only because everything had been turned upside down. That morning all kinds of people were waiting on the doorstep to come inside, people with diverse features, some with hands and feet and a head, all moving at their own pace with their heads down, carrying loaves of bread. They weren't concerned with what day it was, what time it was, whether it was summer or winter. They had managed to procure bread, and that was all that mattered.

Jumaa the Teacher arrived at the Al-Halak shared taxi stand and found a number of cars that were willing to take him to Al-Halak but he told them he wanted to go to the main square via the Tawleed Hospital road. The passenger seated next to him snickered and said, "It's like you don't live here, as if you didn't realize they've blocked off the way into the square via the Tawleed road."

"Who blocked it off?"

"Talk to the driver, maybe he can help you."

Jumaa went to speak with the driver, who had paid him absolutely no attention at first. The driver told him they were going first to al-Shalaal, then directly from there to Shaykh Maqsoud, then they'd turn right, finally heading toward Al-Halak.

"No, no, that's not going to work for me," Jumaa the Teacher said, getting out of the car, deciding to continue his journey on foot instead.

All kinds of gunfire broke out, whether he was in the public gardens or the streets surrounding them. Jumaa the Teacher was stricken with panic, that's right, stricken with panic, or let's call it terror even. Still, sometimes the main squares would dazzle him. He was now bearing witness to clashes between the Muslim Brothers and the regime. He had previously witnessed the 1973 War—he didn't refer to it as the War of Liberation the way the regime did. Maybe that was just inattentiveness, or maybe it was something else.

It's true that he had rounded up the corpses of fighter pilots on the moist earth, sometimes wrapping them with a sheet, but all of that was nothing like what was happening to him now. He looked to the right, where he saw Mukhabarat agents dressed in military fatigues sitting on chairs they had taken from shops that had opened their doors to them in exchange for protection, fanning themselves with scraps of cardboard because the power was out.

And so the calamities continued even as he started to walk, nothing could rattle his confident strides, not the aerial bombardment, the shelling, not the bullets he could hear whizzing past, he didn't care, the goal was clear as day before his eyes, and nothing was going to prevent him from getting there.

Jumaa the Teacher made it near his mother's house, as far as the next neighborhood over, and then his body finally arrived at the street leading to her place.

"You can't go this way," the soldier flatly said, waving a rifle toward him.

I'll take the next street, Jumaa the Teacher decided, but on the next street he found the exact same situation, then on a third street, and so on and so forth, until he reached the produce market at Maysaloun, where he dropped his face into his palm. He wouldn't be able to see the house from there, so he headed west to the Sulaymaniyah neighborhood, where there were women of all ages and shapes and sizes standing in line to buy bread before moving on to buy the rest of their groceries.

When he made it back to the cafe, weighed down by sadness and exhaustion, he sat in the comfortable chair by the window. Suddenly the street burst into action, with gunfire coming from all directions, missiles of every make started to crash down, and as he looked out the window to find out what was happening, he saw a woman using her hand to cover her head and crouching down as she took shelter against the wall. He couldn't quite see what happened next. He gathered all the courage he could muster and rushed into the fray, grabbed her by the hand, and dragged her back with him. Everyone was flying around in a panic, and he ran with her until they made it to the door of the cafe. He shoved her inside and she remained silent.

"I have no idea what they're targeting," he told her, "but they're attacking with full force."

Her face was gaunt, she was depleted and clearly needed someplace to sit down.

"What do you say we go sit in the cafe for a bit?" he asked her, and she nodded at him in agreement.

He walked up the stairs ahead of her and she followed him until they reached his usual table, where some young men he was acquainted with were sitting, so he zigzagged over to another table after saying hello to all of them. He sat down at a table that looked out on Saadallah al-Jabiri Square, from where he could watch everything that was happening directly across from them and out on both sides. She sat down beside him. The sky he looked up at in that moment was as transparent as water. He asked about her situation, what she was doing in such a place at a time like this.

"Nothing, nothing much, they just started attacking," she said curtly, the shock of all the noise clearly affecting her, causing her to behave this way.

Jumaa the Teacher had known Lamya, also a teacher, in a quieter time. He had searched for a new love in her after a previous romance had fallen apart. Early in her time at the school, he had surprised her by walking into the teacher's lounge while she was brushing her hair. He apologized profusely and was about to shut the door on his way out, but she told him to come in, that she was nearly finished. He told a few crass jokes about the situation and she laughed politely. When she finished brushing her hair, she placed her brush and the leather-backed mirror into her purse, then told him she had been dispatched there, to the school that is, as a geography teacher. She had delivered the papers that the superintendent had given her to the headmaster, and then he was visited by two Party cadres while she was asked to wait in the teachers' lounge, and so here she was waiting for the two of them to leave, to finish their necessary activities.

The coffee arrived. We didn't put any sugar into the pot, though the waiter left sugar for us on the table. We ignored it and continued our conversation. I asked her how she and her children were doing. She told me that her eldest daughter had gotten married. When I asked about her husband, she said, with a smile on her face and without clarifying anything for me, that she had packed up all her stuff. Putting out her cigarette she said that it was getting late, and so she stood up to go. I said goodbye to her and she left.

WHY IS IT CALLED
SAADALLAH AL-JABIRI SQUARE?

(From Dr. Muslim al-Zaybaq,
Parties and Political Organizations in the Twentieth Century)

Saadallah al-Jabiri was one of the leaders of the national independence movement. He was born in Aleppo in 1894, where he completed his primary and secondary education, then went on to study at the Imperial Law School in Constantinople, where he was involved in founding the al-Fatat Arab nationalist organization, which called for the independence of the Arab lands and their liberation from the Ottomans. He also participated in the First Arab Congress in 1913.

Saadallah al-Jabiri traveled to Germany for two years, then returned to Constantinople, was conscripted into the Ottoman Army (as a petty officer), and was appointed a commanding officer in Erzurum, where he spent the duration of the First World War.

Afterward he returned to Aleppo and was elected as a member of the First Syrian Congress in 1919. When the northern revolts broke out in 1919, Saadallah al-Jabiri was in contact with the leader of the revolt, Ibrahim Hanano, and al-Jabiri was elected as a member of the constitutional congress from June 9, 1928, until August 11, 1928. He was imprisoned at Arwad Prison for a period of time along with Hashim al-Atassi and a number of other nationalist figures.

At the first Nationalist Congress of the National Bloc in 1932, al-Jabiri was made a minister in the cabinet of President of the National Bloc Hashim al-Atassi, and when the bloc rejected the terms of the 1933 French treaty, demonstrations broke out all over Syria, leading to the arrest of many nationalists, including Saadallah al-Jabiri, who was sentenced to eight years in prison.

Al-Jabiri was elected yet again to the legislative council from July 8, 1939, until December 21, 1939, and he held the position of foreign minister in the first and second administrations of Jamil Mardam Bek. He served as president of the republic three times.

In addition, Saadallah al-Jabiri was head of the Syrian delegation to the signing of the Alexandria Protocols and head of the coordinating committee delegation for the General Arab Conference. Al-Jabiri returned to Aleppo at the end of 1946, and suffering from a chronic illness he went to convalesce in the village of Turaydim, where he died on July 20, 1947. He was buried in Aleppo near the grave of Ibrahim Hanano. There is a statue of him there, in front of the post office, on the right-hand side when one is exiting the building, on the left if one is coming from the Officers' Club.

BOMBING...BOMBING...
DESTRUCTION...DEVASTATION

We endure this horror every day, this raving madness poured into our brains every night, all the people subjected to murder and shelling. The day before as I was leaving Joha's Club I saw a young man being detained by a middle-aged gentleman whom the young man was trying to mollify.

"What have I done? He took my ID card and just started beating me."

"What has he done?" I demanded, and then the man started beating me before I was able to sprint away, then he barked, "Take your ID and get the hell out of here."

Signs of the beating were all over the young man's face and neck. The older man told him to deal with it. He had been coming out of the Officers' Club, where some of the rooms had been transformed into a prison for torturing detainees. We could hear the sound of their screaming voices from the toilet in the cafe, they were hollering and pleading, "Oh God, *hajji*, I'm my mother's only son." The use of that phrase stunned me, proof that the one who was being beaten had never completed his compulsory military service, had never been in the army.

"Shut the fuck up, you sonofabitch," a second voice boomed, and the first voice fell silent for a few seconds.

They had stopped a car outside the business hotel and forced out the driver, demanding his ID card, which he pulled out for them, at which point they piled on top of him and proceeded to beat him senseless, some kicking while others were punching, and those who arrived late just started kicking and punching without knowing why they were doing so. Finally they opened the trunk and shoved him inside, then along came some other unsuspecting person and they did the exact same thing to him that they had done to the first man, shoving him into the trunk as well. We could see all of them through the window.

"They're going to suffocate," one of us exclaimed.

The men outside continued to discuss the matter, then along came a third guy, and after he had been beaten and punched and kicked to their satisfaction, they threw him into the trunk, too.

The important thing, I told myself, is that I go and see my mother. It had been a long time since I last saw her. I made my way out into the square, walked eastward, and before I made it to my mother's house, I turned, in shock, to discover that it looked as though an army had swarmed through there, leaving a trail of destruction in its wake.

The square was nothing like the way I remembered it. The shop doors had been removed or torn off. Here was a building without any windows at all, here's another without balconies, and yet another that was torched, there's one that exploded when a barrel of TNT was dropped on it. I scanned through my mind, wondering whether this was in fact the same square I once knew.

As soon as I knocked on the door, an old lady appeared, someone I barely recognized. My mother had been waiting for me.

"Thank God the entire house wasn't destroyed," I said.

"You say that now, but take a closer look," she said, showing me around.

It appeared to be totally ruined from the outside—no windows and no shutters, absolutely nothing left. Inside, the house was full of dust and rubble and rocks both big and small.

"Your tragedy isn't so bad compared to others," I offered.

"You always minimize the scale of tragedy," she rebutted.

Both of us were silent. I sat there with her for about an hour. A fighter jet was circling high overhead until it zoomed toward us and dropped its payload. I grabbed my mother's hand and pushed her deeper inside the house, into a room where she wouldn't be exposed to any shelling. I glanced over at the neighbor's balcony that had been hit. Everyone was pointing toward it as I left. The next day the sun was shining brightly in the street. I walked out of the house and saw the driver of a yellow car picking out glass from the rear window.

"Everything okay, I hope?" I asked him.

He told me they had been in Saadallah al-Jabiri Square when the explosion took place.

"Which explosion are you talking about?"

"Like I said, there was an explosion in the square, and I was able to get away because I was on the outskirts."

I headed over to the square, or just a bit outside the square, into the Jumayliyah neighborhood. They prevented me from getting any closer. Even from afar I could see trucks carting away the debris. When I finally made it home, I was horrified by what I found. Saadallah al-Jabiri Square had been obliterated. The business hotel now looked like an old man staring at his own grave. There no longer remained anything called Joha's Club, not even the building that once housed it. The cellular company MTN and the mobile accessories store and the Officers' Club: all of them were gone, nothing remained. Those of us who had been dispersed from there, would we ever meet again?

THE ISLAND CAFE

The Island Cafe where we reconstituted ourselves is nicer than Joha's Club, which had been wiped off the map of Aleppo. Here is where we'll sit from this day forward, and we'll appreciate its location, which is right next to the Al-Siddiq mosque, you could say it's not much more than two hundred meters from there. There were no more encampments in Saadallah al-Jabiri Square, the business hotel had to move everything out of the building, and their cafe had been wiped out of existence. The Officers' Club, meanwhile, was no longer a functioning club, the section underneath the cafe was gone altogether and could no longer accommodate anybody. They had brought some soldiers over to work security for the building, and soon it was totally forbidden to walk through the square. I could no longer see the pine trees and their boughs that craned up toward the sky in order to tell their stories and inhale some clean air. I could no longer see the tops of the trees as they embraced one another when the breeze caused them to sway to and fro. All of that was gone, gone for good.

The city was divided in half and those two halves never intersected. One half, the east, was demarcated by the square as well as the Shaykh Abu Bakr and Maysaloun neighborhoods. The other half was marked by the death roundabout, to the west. All forms of communication had been severed between east and west. Aleppo was besieged. Food supplies, including fresh fruits and vegetables, could no longer get into the city. Urban dwellers were forced to begin trading with the other half of the city. A public market sprang up, where the entire portion of the city that was with the regime went to buy goods, where they would find little carts transporting home furnishings, sacks of produce, other foodstuffs, and dead bodies. You set off from there, from Al-Fayd to Al-Kuttab, and from there through the regime checkpoint over to the no-man's land, then onward to a zone controlled by the Free Syrian Army or Jabhat al-Nusra. People would depart with empty hands, much like their carts that carried nothing but the dead wrapped in white shrouds, sheets over the top, and all around there were shouts for everyone to give way to the dead, declaring that there is only one true God and no other. The dead would cross over to the next world without anyone reciting the Fatiha over their souls because of the rush to shove the crowds aside. You would have to hustle if you were walking on foot, and as you crossed the river you might be met with sniper fire. There could be one stationed up on the roof of the Ameer Hotel, to the east, and another on top of the television station, to the west. Both of them would shoot at people—*taaaaakhkh*, a civilian drops to the ground and a group of mujahideen or a bunch of people with Jabhat al-Nusra would rush over and carry the wounded away to an ambulance by their hands and feet. They equipped the spot near the checkpoint crossing with a rudimentary ambulance, one doctor and one nurse on hand, to treat anyone injured by sniper fire, although most of the time these cases resulted in death.

One time when I was going to Damascus there was shelling going on, more like an exchange of gunfire. The shelling continued as we boarded a bus. We sped off to the checkpoints that would prevent us from going any further right away. Whenever we stopped at a roadblock, a militiaman would come on board to check IDs, scrutinizing our faces and then looking back down at our identity cards, before disembarking from the bus with a fresh bottle of water or however much money could be filched. Then we reached the Al-Qateefa checkpoint, where the bus attendant gathered up all of our IDs and left the vehicle. Running all of our names through the computer took nearly half an hour, then the bus took off once again, until we arrived in Homs, which we found was a shattered city, full of squawking birds, including crows and owls in the sky, with rats, mice, and all kinds of scavengers down on the ground. We passed through various checkpoints before reaching the part of Homs that was still inhabited by human beings. People were having coffee on their balconies, women were out buying vegetables, and men were walking around looking pleased as punch, as my beloved students might put it in composition class. Life was carrying on as usual. Meanwhile, in the destroyed part of Homs you'd find checkpoints and soldiers, and declarations of: "Halt! No Photography Allowed," and "Halt! This Is a Checkpoint," as soldiers collected all the things that people had left behind when they fled the eye of the storm.

We left Homs toward the east, on a national highway, because on all the international roads there were attacks that were, to put it mildly, crushing. We crept eastward toward Salamiyah, where there was an armed checkpoint waiting for us. When the bus attendant handed them hundreds of liras, we were able to zip right through as delight spread across our faces, that is, until we reached the international road at Maarat al-Numan, on which we drove for six hours, maybe more.

As soon as we had passed Maarat al-Numan, the driver stepped on the gas, and the bus took us to Al-Zirbah, where we arrived at precisely 5:00. My house is close to there, not more than fifteen minutes by car, only now we'll see how long it takes us. By the time the van had picked up all its passengers, it was already 5:30, and the driver took off without much regard for anything, and if he did pay attention to anything it was just to stare back at us and smile. He turned left to pass through Khan al-Asal and whatever villages and neighborhoods were nearby, continuing onto the Castello Road, descending to Bab al-Nayrab, then Al-Kalasa, and Al-Maabar. The trip took nearly three hours and fifteen minutes; one that used to take me fifteen minutes now required three more hours of our time. I picked up my bag and started walking, turning my face toward what remained of the house when the first bombs landed near me. These weren't RPG rockets as far as I could tell, these might have been tank armaments. Heavy shelling exploded throughout the streets and the neighborhoods and the alleyways.

Fighters with long beards said: "They've shut down the crossing point and started to set up barricades in building entryways." All the street vendors had closed up shop. People who were hunkered down inside behind the walls started to say: "There is no God but God, Muhammad is the Messenger of God." Bombs rained down on buildings, the streets thundered with sounds I had never heard before. The roads were empty, even cats had retreated into locations where they wouldn't be hit. There was a pile of rubble between me and the khan, a large courtyard inn which was more like a hangar, but who would be able to pass and get across? There were blown-out buildings, a broad street, and Bab al-Khan, where long-bearded militiamen had taken cover behind the walls, preventing people from passing. Those guys had decided to use the bombs to kill people, heavy shells fell all over the place like raindrops, preventing anyone from getting anywhere even as those men shouted that the checkpoint was closed. An image flickered in my memory for a moment: my journey to Damascus. I had left there the day before at eight in the morning, and now it was 8:45 the next day. I remembered the bombardment of the garages, the place at the end of Al-Qaboon where the buses were parked, and the man who had been wounded in the hand and had to have it amputated. There had been very few passengers on our bus, they might have been from Hassakeh. I remembered the blood that spurted from his amputated hand. They wrapped his wrist with a handkerchief like a tourniquet, took the hand with them and ran over to the car that would rush them to the hospital, and the driver shot off to get us to the checkpoint, the ID check, and the bus inspection, the taking of money and water from the bus attendant, and after we had set off from the rest stop near Hama we reached the zone controlled by the Free Syrian Army, finally arriving at Maaret al-Numan, Al-Zirbah, and then the shared taxi, which finally brought me here.

I was with people who were saying that death is real. I prayed for my soul as the bombs fell upon us. I didn't know anyone in the FSA-controlled area, otherwise I would have stayed the night with them. There are some relatives of mine around there, but as soon as I stepped out of the building where I had taken shelter someone from the FSA or maybe someone else shouted at me to get back inside, which I did. I tried to think if there was anyone in this neighborhood with whom I could find refuge but couldn't come up with a single name. Night started to fall on all the people and the streets and the buildings. Although this neighborhood had no electricity, I was still able to see. Eventually I needed to do something: either leave the place where I was and go backward or else . . .

An idea flashed in my mind. The sniping had lightened up a bit, so I sneaked into the khan and crossed the street over to the other side.

It took a great deal of courage for me to pull this off, especially as the shelling got worse, and I encouraged myself, "Let those who trust in God trust in God." I eased myself through the entrance without anyone seeing me because the militiamen were still taking cover behind the walls. Step by step I made it back out to the boulevard, then the khan, which I hurried through, until I reached the second gate, muttering to myself, "Scram, all of you, I'm king of the world, just like Al-Zeir Salem." Then I started running. Was there a single combatant who could defeat me? Were there any fighters? Ten against one, a hundred on one, a thousand to one. I ran as fast as I could while shouting out loud, Is there anyone here who can best me? Only the place itself responded to me, there was nobody around, only desolate shadows accompanied me as I moved along the edge of the government employees' hospital, where human blood had been splattered all over the walls from sniper fire. I screamed again and the place responded with silence and gloom, so I pumped my legs even harder and shouted, I'm Abu Zayd al-Hilali, is there anyone who can defeat me? Now I had reached the river, which informed me, *You are blessed, my son, there is nobody here, continue on your way.*

And so I walked on worry-free, crossed over the other street, slipped beneath the buildings, and when I reached the military security checkpoint, my soul had drifted off somewhere far away from me, I caught a glimpse of it high up in the sky before pulling it back down and stuffing it inside of me. Then I crossed the next street, walking with my head held high. I saw people behind me, men and women who seemed to be weighed down as they ran. I walked right through the checkpoint without anyone noticing. I passed right through. There were some men in camouflage gathered together with women in military uniforms, deep in conversation about something or other.

My suitcase was tucked under my arm as I continued making my way, and I started to sing, "He's brave in his power, he's so very, very brave," moving down the empty street until I reached the Al-Fayd neighborhood, where there was a bus hauling people to New Aleppo in the south, so I hopped on and waited until the driver was ready to go. He was smoking, flicking cigarette ashes out the window, and then he started to drive us away as he bellowed, "Southbound! Southbound!" My soul had been weighing heavily upon me and it now felt as though I were relaxing with my feet in cool water as he crossed Al-Fayd to the Le Meridien hotel and continued on to the university, stopping there and shouting out once again, "Southbound . . . Southbound," picking up additional passengers and then taking us toward Al-Kura Al-Ardiyah, then to the Al-Furqan neighborhood, and finally arriving at the death roundabout, where I got off to walk on foot. I counted five buildings, then veered off toward the right and entered a building, climbed up to the second floor, took out the keys, and opened the door. I had arrived in one piece.

FROM THE TOTALLY DECIMATED
JOHA'S CLUB TO THE ISLAND CAFE

Most of the group who used to hang out at Joha's Club shifted over to the Island Cafe, which was located behind the Al-Siddiq mosque, well, actually it was inside the Islamic religious endowment office building behind the mosque, that gargantuan complex situated between the post office and the mosque, composed of multiple buildings that included offices and residential apartments, all of which were empty, nobody had set foot inside for a while, built on the red earth that is the stomping ground of the Assads, the earth we used to boast about during the June 1967 war, chanting, "They called us! They called us! To Palestine they sent us." In those days the military police pounded us, beat us with truncheons and belts as we pelted them with stones. All that came to an end when an official representative from the People's Army came out to meet us, and as far as we high school students were concerned, we were beholden to him, and he spoke and announced to those listening that they should come back the next day, when there'd be weapons and training and a journey to Palestine. Nobody showed up.

Construction on this red-earthed land had been supervised by the Directorate of Pious Endowments, but they wouldn't let anybody live there, except in special cases for those who had a lot of money and wanted to set up a shop on the ground floor of the building, including this Island Cafe.

Truth be told the Island Cafe was a pleasure to frequent. We'd sit there in the summertime when the trees spread shade all over, especially in the morning. It was located on the road that led to the education ministry, and from there on to the electric company, then the public garden where we could no longer look at tall trees or flowers to brighten our mood or even fountains because there wasn't any water. In that new cafe of ours I would sit and watch doves flitting between the tall trees, but now there were no more doves, no more public garden, no more Saadallah al-Jabiri Square, no more business hotel. All of those things were now in the past. The hotel had been leveled and its remains had been spat out in one blow. The park had shut its gates, except for the east and west entrances, and anyone who entered or exited was searched by the militia of the ruling party, with more than ten of its men stationed at each point, dressed in camouflage uniforms and tattered athletic shoes—they'd apathetically rummage around for nothing in particular—feeling under people's armpits and around their waists and across their chests, down their legs to the feet and then back up again in between. If you were carrying a bag of food, they'd search that, too, which is why walking alongside the garden outside became more enjoyable than going inside. Here in the cafe adjacent to the park they handed out food to people who had none, regardless of whether they were with the Party or the revolution, each with a bowl in their hand, and they'd ladle out *mujadara* stew and slop it into the bowl. There were droves of people lined up and waiting to fill their bowls.

The Island Cafe is divided into three parts: a summer section, a winter section, and a rooftop. There is WiFi for customers with smartphones, who pull them out and make calls while they're there.

Typically, there aren't too many of us, ten people or so, give or take, including a doctor, a lawyer, and an unemployed teacher. Some are retired, some own their own businesses, some of us have lost our children and some are just waiting for no reason at all.

We moved from the summer room into the winter room because of shelling from a 14-millimeter machine gun that had incinerated the roof, causing it to come crashing down between Jamal and Anwar, who quipped that the summer room was no longer suitable for us, and therefore shuffled into the winter room in summer and winter alike. The second table from the door was for us, the word *Reserved* was posted on it until we arrived. One or two of us might be absent, maybe more, this was never an issue, or there could be more than that many missing, no problem there either.

Whenever the water is interrupted throughout the city, or even if it's only in the Jumayliyah neighborhood, you'll find people coming with their barrels and carts and plastic tanks, queuing up in long lines in order to fill up. The cafe has an artesian well where people can take as much water as they need and then be on their way. All of this is well-organized, and even though the water isn't treated, they'll tell you at the cafe that they have asked doctors who say it's safe to drink. Now I—and I beg God's forgiveness for repeating the term *I* here—am no longer waiting for the woman who may or may not ever come walking through the door. I have been waiting for her for seven long years, and I had to give up my habit of waiting back there at Joha's Club. There is no use in waiting here because this isn't an elevated place from which one can look out on the square, and there isn't a clear path toward West Aleppo the way there is at Joha's: no tents, no shabbiha sleeping inside. Saadallah al-Jabiri Square is totally deserted. All of the tents have been taken down, each and every party has pulled up its tent stakes and moved on, the singer with the mellifluous voice is gone, we never see her anymore, and those who used to pass through the square now pass along the edges, coming from the direction of the public park, for example, but hurrying along on their way.

At our cafe, by which I now mean the Island Cafe, you'll find an upper level, which is a cafe for families. The tables will be mostly filled with young ladies and young men smoking water pipes and having something to drink, you'll find the place dense with smoke from all of the *argileh* and because the women inhale so deeply and blow out such huge quantities of smoke until their eyes get all bloodshot and their cheeks turn flush, as they expel the smoke from their mouths that begin to resemble metallic censers.

The shabbiha who frequent the cafe never sit down, they simply stand there smoking and clutching their rifles, then leave with their coffee, and even though some might hover over us for a while, we don't pay them any mind.

I consider myself part of the opposition, which means I'm opposed to anyone who sits with me: if they say that *laban* is white, I say it's black, if they say the sky is black then I tell them it's white as milk. It all started at a restaurant one evening when the uprising first began, back when I was still supportive of the revolution. Whenever I went to visit my mother in the Midan neighborhood, I'd see them outside the Al-Burj restaurant getting ready for Friday prayer, fifteen or twenty cars, some pickup trucks, some taxis. In every car and in every pickup truck there was a group of shabbiha inside and an officer behind the wheel, some had dogs with them, the least one could say of those animals is that they were wild. Now they were getting ready for deployment, awaiting orders. It's possible they were nervous, feeling anxiety and trepidation, popping pills to give themselves energy and confidence: here's one taking two tablets, downing them quickly, here's another shoving one down his throat surreptitiously so that his supervising officer won't notice, even as the commander retreats into his room where he also takes a pill, until everyone is flying through his own universe.

Another officer was dragging a bare-naked and bleeding young man by his bloody shirt, which had been yanked up and wrapped around his neck, as he punched and slapped his exposed back. He threw him between two men in a taxi and they drove off when the orders came to depart, which is when the caravan of death set off, as Mahmoud called it, sitting at the Al-Burj restaurant. Somebody shouted at them and the officer drove off. You could easily tell his rank because he was driving a white Kia taxi. The rest of them were in pickup trucks. Anyone with a car had filled it with fearsome fighters, and as the caravan inched away, they honked their horns and fired their guns all over the place. They left with their handguns and rifles, their wild dogs, their metal chains and their batons, their heads shaved, and they set off toward one of the mosques, surrounded it, and savagely beat anyone who came out, those who had just finished Friday prayer and were now chanting at the top of their lungs, "Freedom! Freedom! The People Want Freedom!"

I no longer go to my mother's house on Fridays. We agreed that I would go see her another day instead because we have trouble on Friday: demonstrations and car bombings are always taking place on Friday, also there are ID checks for every citizen, detainments and cell phone confiscations; no matter what, they say, take him to the car, by which they mean a paddy wagon with bars on the windows, like a prison cell, which quickly fills up with people, at which point the commanding officer calls for them to bring another vehicle. So I decided to leave Fridays to others and sit home instead, making all different kinds of *ful* bean stew: ful with tahina, ful with hummus, with a few falafel balls: I'd spread all the dishes out on the table with chopped tomato, parsley, mint, lettuce, laban, and olive oil, and then we'd all start eating. My son loves to drink tea with breakfast on Fridays, he'll boil and brew the tea himself, and he doesn't like to have ful without a cup of tea, one during breakfast and another one afterward. If the electricity happens to come on, we'll all pile in front of the television to watch Al-Arabiya or Al-Jazeera, which air demonstrations taking place all over the country. Then my son will perform his ablutions and, in the politest way possible, tell me, "I'm off to pray." "Pray for us," I'd tell him, "so that God may forgive us all." He'd head out without responding and breakfast would be cleared from the table.

When I went to visit my mother, she told me my sister Shukriya had fled to stay here, by which she meant on regime-controlled territory.

"Her house is near Sulayman Al-Halabi, across from what's its name, I can't remember exactly, fourth floor."

Shukriya is my sister by a different mother. I told my mother I'd go see her.

"Why don't we go together?" I asked her. She liked the idea and got ready to leave.

We passed through the Sulayman Al-Halabi neighborhood on the way to Al-Musawwar, the building whose name my mother had forgotten, and we walked up to the fourth floor. Her house was on the front line, starting here is the regime, and from there, just behind her building, is the Free Syrian Army. I rang the bell but didn't hear a sound. My mother said the power was out.

"Oh yeah," I said. "I completely forgot."

I knocked on the door instead, and my sister's daughter appeared, shouting, "Who is it?"

After recognizing her grandmother, she spun around to tell her mother that her grandmother and I had come to visit. My kindly sister welcomed us as we stepped inside. She was my sister by my father, who had married two different women, my mother and my mother's sister. My mother is the new wife, while my aunt is the old one. My father would sleep one night at the old wife's, one night at the new wife's. My oldest sister is this one called Shukriya, or Umm Abduh, and she had given birth to thirteen children, eleven boys and two girls. They were a badge of distinction for her, meaning, for example, she wouldn't pay the bus fare when the driver asked for it, just turn up her nose and say, "Badge of honor," and the driver would move along to the next person.

My sister kissed us both on the cheeks and asked us to have a seat in her one-room apartment. In a whisper she informed us how her children and all of their children had stayed behind, by which she meant back there in the Al-Kalasa neighborhood. She could no longer stand the fighter jets dropping barrel bombs on them every day, even the ones that never exploded. She followed the news about the barrels closely: the day before, Abu Muhammad's shops had been hit, and the day before that, some other person's building had been shelled. Then she began to tell us all about the barrels that exploded as well as those that didn't, until her older son finally advised her to leave for regime-controlled territory, and so he packed up a moving truck with foam bedding and blankets, and told her, "Go with God."

My sister explained how she had to travel for seven hours, on the Minbaj Road to Khansir, then to Al-Safira before looping back to Aleppo. That route should have taken no longer than the time it takes to cross over al-Fayd Street, but now amounts to seven hours of travel. There were checkpoints waiting for us as well, she told us, somebody would demand to know, who are you? When they told him they were from Al-Kalasa, they were instructed to get out of the van so it could be searched thoroughly, and when the soldiers didn't find anything of interest inside, they ordered them to proceed, until they reached the checkpoint at the Four Minarets Mosque, where they told them to get out once again so the van could be searched, turned upside down really, but still they didn't find anything. They denied them entry nevertheless, and my sister said how they would keep you waiting, telling you it would be this long and then that long, and they ended up waiting there for nearly two hours before there was a shift change and they were cleared to leave.

When they finally made it over here, my sister, her daughter, her son's wife as well as another son along with his sixteen-year-old son, they rented an apartment, this single room and its facilities. Every day they could hear shooting and bombardment, until they became accustomed to all of that, until it no longer seemed to faze them at all, as my sister said.

She quietly told us about how her grandson had volunteered for the popular fighting brigades, how he was transformed into a fighter after they provided him with a rifle, three grenades, ammunition, a uniform, and payment in advance, and how he had then been deployed east of Al-Safira to Al-Ta'aneh, where he was sent to fight terrorists. My sister meekly smiled in shame when she described to me how two of her children had joined up with the mujahideen in Jabhat al-Nusra, while another one had volunteered with the FSA, and all of them were now fighting in the area east of Al-Safira.

We fell back into our own thoughts as we sipped the tea the little girl brought us. Once my mother was safely back home, I took a shared taxi to my place. But before I had made it as far as the Basil al-Assad statue, I noticed people starting to congregate, sitting on chairs along both sides of the street, some of them munching on seeds, some chomping on lettuce, while women were busy making tabbouleh. I thought to myself: people are like this, people are like that, people could no longer expect grilled meat, they made do with green beans, tabbouleh, and lettuce. They say that it's better for the body and your health. And so they walk for exercise as well, there are three girls walking over here and four more over there, two young men wearing camouflage, a trailer truck parked over here, a Suzuki over there, street vendors hawking coffee with creamer, tea, Milo chocolate malt, and another selling spirits lined up all along the length of the monument.

"Brother, they've divided the country among themselves. Every rooster crows on his own garbage heap now. They won't let you crow anymore, and if anyone does, then every-one has to line up behind one another while they check IDs. If there's a fruit or vegetable cart they'll just dump whatever they can into the guard station. If a Suzuki happens to be car-rying home furniture, have pity for them as the men bark at them to pull over and leave their car off to the side, demand-ing, "Where are your documents?" The driver has to step out with the car's registration. "Where are you coming from?" And then there are more questions that ultimately lead to the driver *donating* a thousand liras to the checkpoint, and then it's all "Drive on, move along."

My sister didn't realize any of this until she got stopped at the checkpoint and had to wait for two hours, pulled aside with those she was traveling with. Their journey would have been much simpler if she had simply handed over the money at the outset. My sister was inexperienced, she had come from FSA territory, and all of their names were entered into a computer when they reached the Al-Ramouseh neighbor-hood, as she told me and my mother, where she was detained at that motherfucking checkpoint, as she called it. My sister Shukriya dropped out of school because there were adult men and young boys there. School was forbidden for girls because they would have to sit in the same class with boys. My sister got married when she was young. My aunt came—well, not my mother's sister, but the sister of my aunt who had mar-ried my father, the old wife—along with her husband, son, and daughter, and they all sat down in the great room in our house to get her engaged. She hadn't even turned fifteen years old, and within three months her fiancé and his brother were able to cobble together the dowry that we used to buy a gown, some bedding, and to pay for the wedding party. The bride didn't cry before the rest of us did on this blessed occasion, and she left our care so quickly. They took the bride to the bathhouse, to the Al-Effendi Hammam, and I was in the lead among those who escorted her over there.

The Al-Effendi Hammam is located at the end of the Al-Zahr souq, the market that specializes in selling beauty supplies, textiles, and other essentials for a traditional wedding. The Al-Effendi Hammam is to the east, and directly in front of it is the rear entrance of the Al-Zahr Hammam, which looks out on the Bab Al-Hadid plaza, but the rear of the building had been transformed into a flea market.

WE GRILL AND GRILL AND DON'T EVEN MAKE BACK THE COST OF THE COALS

I went down to the vegetable sellers in the Bab Al-Hadid souq. They were selling grilled meat from carts, one with kebab on skewers and another where they were grilling on hot coals, the first on a cart where they cubed the minced meat and speared it onto a stick, the cook's voice booming throughout the space, "We grill and grill and don't even make back the cost of the meat!" Out front there was a platter decorated with parsley and onion and tomato. There were parsley sprigs on top of the cart, and off to the right there was finely chopped tomato. He'd slide a skewer or two in between a piece of pita bread and then cover it with *biwaz* salad, tomato, and a little bit of salt and crushed pepper for anyone who wanted some. One customer took the sandwich to his Bedouin wife, who was sitting far away from the crowd, and then returned to get himself one. He had promised her that if they ever had the chance to visit Aleppo, he would make sure she tasted the kebab. He returned to her with the second wrap and the two of them ate together in silence.

Little birds of hunger started chirping in my belly. I had one-quarter of a lira so I stopped and bought a sandwich for ten *qurush*, sprinkling a bit of crushed pepper over the top. I nibbled on some radishes as I ate my sandwich. The whole operation amazed me. I asked the griller whether he needed any help.

"Ask the boss," he grunted, so I did.

After scrutinizing me closely, he said, "Come back tomorrow. You'll take home three liras per week. Don't snack on the meat or anything else. Bring some tap water with you and wash the skewers before you leave. Your shift will be from 8:00 a.m. until the meat runs out."

I told him I could start working that day and he told me to go ahead.

I filled the water jug from the tap at the mosque and filled a second jug for drinking, then immediately started shouting out, "Grilled meat, grilled meat!" I took the fan from Abu Muhammad, who was blowing it on the skewered meat. I stashed a cigarette behind my ear and started shifting the coals around, putting some fresh pieces on top of the lit ones, which increased the strength of the embers. I split open the smoldering coals and laid the skewers on the grill while he smoked a cigarette and sipped a cup of tea. As he poured the boss a glass I pulled the cigarette out from behind my ear and lit it up, grilling the tomato and the onion and the hot pepper. "Grilled meat! Grilled meat!" I shouted. "We don't even make back the cost of the coals . . . step right up, step right up, dear friends!"

Soon the cart was jammed with customers eating as I grilled the huge amount of meat that Abu Muhammad had provided me, and by 3:00 p.m. the meat had run out along with the salad and all the tomatoes, so I put away the supplies and washed everything down with the water I had brought with me. Then I placed the kettle on the fire, and when it started to boil I hurried over with cups, blew on the fire until it was extinguished, washed all the silverware and the plates, well, not *washed* exactly the way my skillful sister would, you might say I scraped off the parsley and most of the grease from the silverware, then placed it all inside the cart and shut the doors tight.

"Be here early tomorrow," the boss ordered me.

"What about my pay?" I asked.

He laughed jovially, the first time I had seen him laugh all day, then he reached his hand into his pocket, pulled out half a lira and handed it to me. I thanked him. I had stashed a piece of bread and some salad over by the mosque, so I hurried over there, but the bread was gone. When I noticed a street kid was eating it, I rushed at him, kicked him, grabbed the bread from out of his hand, but then handed him back a quarter of it. He took it from me and continued eating, so I ate there with him before heading back toward the souq.

I made my way to the Al-Mashatiyah market, passing by an omelet stand, where I stopped for a moment and asked the cook to make me some eggs. He cracked one on the side of a bowl and dropped the egg inside, sprinkled parsley and chopped onion on top, then some salt and other spices, mixed it all together and poured in a little water so that it would set, and put the whole mixture into the pan. He tossed a piece of wood underneath, poked it around with a fire iron, then stood back up all chalky and swollen, looking hilarious. He tore up a piece of bread and scattered the morsels into the eggs, adding some pickled vegetables for me, which made everyone's mouths start to water. Then he mixed in cucumber and spicy peppers. I took my food and walked up the end of the street, where I sat down and started to devour it with uncharacteristic appetite.

I finished the entire sandwich and a couple loaves of pita bread, which left me with one more round and a couple large chunks. I decided to hold onto them for my skillful sister, since she was bound to be hungry from her long day of work, but then I thought better of it when I remembered that my sister was getting married, surely they would bring home some good food, so I bundled up the food and started singing to myself, "O silver heart, why are you so angry, I'd give anything for your forgiveness, brother, from the spring of my . . . from the spring of my . . ." I struggled to complete the song, "Olive Green" by Lena Chamamyan, but I couldn't remember the words, and as hard as I tried to stoke my memory, it was no use, so I gave up and improvised the words, "the spring of my balls . . ."

After my sister Shukriya got married, her husband would bring her around every month, then every two months, then every major holiday. Her husband worked in construction, building the horizontal beams of each floor so that young men could come along and pour concrete on top, then he would level out the bathrooms and the ceilings, stabilizing the beams and building the staircases.

"Give me the construction joint, quick, boy!" And the boy handed over the joint. "And bring some wood, boy!" And the boy brought the wood. He was an expert in his craft, and had no equal. He recruited his brother to the work so that he, too, could learn the craft that would keep them out of poverty. His brother was the apprentice, and Shukriya's husband was the master. He would place the beams, the extra wood, and the stoppers beside the house, and he nailed them all together, all of that for Friday, the day when the two of them would pour the foundation for houses without permits. It was only a few years before the two of them managed to buy a piece of land, where her husband poured concrete and built a house, bringing in electricity and water, and every year they'd build a little more, until it became a building on the side of the street, a sight to all who passed by. But her husband was shot in the neck by sniper fire and fell down without saying another word. He had been standing with his wife Shukriya as the two of them were preparing red peppers when the hit came, *BANG*, and his entire body collapsed to the ground, and from that point the eastern section of the city became a shooting range for barrel bombs, and ever since then the family had been divided into one group fighting with the FSA, and others fighting alongside regime forces, which deeply saddened Shukriya, causing her to retreat inside of herself, the family no longer held itself together, their father got killed or was martyred, and all the children wound up opposing one another.

"Trust in God," I told my sister, "He won't forget about you."

When my skillful sister reached the age of consent, she then got engaged to one of her cousins. He didn't come by himself to do the deed, but sent his mother and father to see us instead.

"But your son is already married," my father protested.

His mother said he would only be happy if he had a proper heir, he wants a son, may God provide for your children in due time, it's because his wife has only been able to give birth to daughters, three girls in five years.

My father replied that we would discuss the matter and send them our decision, and he did discuss the matter with my sister's mother. This cousin is a big deal in his region, he's very well off, the girl would never go hungry, my father told her, but she would always be the second wife. My mother said that they all marry their own women, the idea being that those you already know are preferable to those you haven't met yet. At this point my skillful sister got involved, declaring her intention to marry him.

"But he already has a wife," my father said, "and you'll always be the second wife."

"I know," she said flatly, before walking out of the room.

And so they sent word to the house of the future groom, "Come and fetch your bride."

My skillful sister married her new groom, and for seven days his other wife remained elsewhere with her daughters at her side. On the eighth day he brought her and her daughters back to the house so that they could move on with their lives. As soon as her husband left for the cafe, my skillful sister pulled out her vanity kit and began putting on makeup. This was in the courtyard of the large house, across from the building where she lived. She pulled out her tweezers and started plucking her eyebrows, then she filed her nails, and before her husband got back home, her co-wife took a tank of gasoline, stood in the middle of the courtyard, poured the liquid all over herself, and began hurling insults at my sister. Her daughters all started sobbing as they watched this happen. My sister carried on with what she was doing with remarkable aplomb even as the other woman wailed and shouted at my sister for having stolen her husband. My sister hardly noticed what she was saying, just kept filing her nails, and when their husband opened the door, she cried out to him, "Look at this mess you've made, Abu Samira!" then grabbed a box of matches and lit herself on fire. Abu Samira rushed toward her but she was already a ball of roaring fire, he couldn't even get close to her, he was shouting and howling, then grabbed a bucket of water and dumped it on the mother of his daughters, but the flames just grew higher because of her synthetic clothing.

The girls were terrified, all of them were bawling, clinging to one another, but my sister didn't move a muscle, just sat there with the nail polish applicator in her hand, holding onto her toes as if nothing had happened, while the other woman, the mother of those daughters, was moaning, and then fell to the ground in silence. Her husband wrapped her up in a sheet and rushed her to the hospital, where he filled out a report attesting that this woman had died by incineration. She was later buried in the Sheikh Yousef cemetery, with a funeral attended by her relatives as well as her husband's relatives, those who were still alive anyway, good people of the community, those with kind hearts. They recited the Verse of Yas, then the Fatiha prayer, and then everyone mourned. Their husband's brother paid for everything, whether that meant compensating the ones who buried the corpse or those who had helped out in other ways, to say nothing of the money they handed out to beggars they encountered along the way. Meanwhile, my sister switched on the hot water heater, sent the three daughters to their grandmother's and finished filing her nails, then she went into the bathroom and got ready to welcome her husband back, and when he opened the door and realized his wife was inside, he announced that he was home.

After getting married my sister enjoyed a happy and comfortable life while her husband's mother raised his daughters. My sister only gave birth to one son, who was stocky and broad-shouldered, his hands big enough to work like a bulldozer, and her husband truly was a big deal, in the morning she'd watch him getting dressed in expensive traditional Arab garb: a heavy robe with a vest and a jacket, a Persian shawl around his shoulders, and some metalware around his neck. He asked his wife to make sure he looked all right, and after she gave him a once-over and offered her comments on his outfit, he'd make his way to the cafe. He gave some cash to a sheepish-looking guy who would go and buy meat, vegetables, and whatever else they needed at the house. The man didn't do anything at all at home, my sister took care of everything: she prepared the hashish and filled small sacks with it, the weight of each one was precisely half a kilogram, then she'd pack them into boxes, and finally seal them all up. Her husband was in charge of distributing the product, mostly it was once a month, when young men would come knocking on the door of the guest house, asking him, Hey Uncle, and after all the late-night visitors had been exhausted a small shipping van would show up to carry away the boxes that had been stamped with my sister's professional seal, Shamsa, and they'd wait until morning to drive that van over to the depot. Shamsa's husband had bought off the police and security services so that when the van set out in the morning, the streets would be empty, there would be no police or security forces, and nobody to be concerned about what was happening.

When Shamsa's son got older, he showed absolutely no interest in the family business, he was much more into trading antiquities and rare manuscripts. He would spend his days hunting them down, purchasing whatever he could. He didn't sell those items inside the country, though, he would send them to Lebanon, where they would be catalogued and sent for international auction in London.

He looked out for himself, started spending a lot of time with high-level officers and the heads of security stations, government ministers, people like that. His property on the Damascus Road became a meeting spot where they would stay up late into the night partying, bringing in whiskey and women, and anyone who wished to take a girl to a bedroom could experience whatever they wanted. The most desirable women would show up there along with men who held all kinds of positions of authority, people well known for smuggling hashish, pills, and liquor, judges and high-ranking police officials, security services bigwigs and tribal leaders, all sorts of people from the city. You certainly might say that they were creating a house of cards for themselves, abetting one another by not asking about any crimes being committed, just going ahead and committing them, and for that reason you might also say that they were able to monopolize the black market. They didn't lack for anything. They simply did as they pleased.

TAKE ME WITH YOU TO EUROPE

Everyone was silent at the Island Cafe, ours was the only table where people were talking. Nader the unemployed lawyer had gotten there first, his cell phone glued to his hand as he talked to the whole world over Facebook; then Nizar, a doctor who was unemployed, too, but only because he had retired, sold his practice, and was waiting for his pension checks to start arriving—he was also on Facebook at that moment—and Muhammad D, a novelist, or at least the author of one novel, although the circumstances weren't helping him finish his second, was sitting there staring off toward the east. We'd always find him sitting there with two briefcases, and we never knew what was in either one. The barista called him Doctor because he knew more about medicine than many physicians, he'd show up for doctor's visits carrying medical journals to discuss with them, and often when he popped over to the pharmacy for a few minutes to pick up a prescription, he'd tell the person next to him to keep an eye on his cell phone that was charging, and that person would tell him not to worry. He'd spend a few minutes in the pharmacy then return to his phone, look at it for a moment only to discover that it hadn't recharged yet. He slept in the Al-Musharaqah neighborhood, on the front line between the old and the new city, and every night he spent there he would hear people cursing at one another, or degrading other men's wives, hurling insults every which way. Mahmoud also came around from time to time, bringing us books to read, but usually nothing more than that. Newspapers no longer found their way to us. We used to solve crossword puzzles in the papers at Joha's Club. But they don't make it to the cafe anymore so we can no longer do the crosswords.

The young men who are left come around on Monday, Thursday, and Saturday, and they don't make any trouble, they just show up, drink their coffee, talk some politics, and then leave.

There's an aid distribution center next to the cafe where you'll find hordes and hordes of people who come to pick up five yellow bottles of vegetable oil; a blanket and a foam mattress for every member of the household; a razor blade, toothbrush, toothpaste, rice, tea, and a few other things I may have forgotten. I'll go see about it tomorrow, then I'll be sure to write it down.

I—and I cautiously speak in the name of *I*—come by the cafe every day, sit down, and observe. I'm inspired by an artist who paints here and sends some of his paintings to Saudi Arabia, leaving some here, hopeful that somebody might buy them someday. This artist has a narrow mind, replying to any question without giving the answer much thought. You go east, he goes west, or he'll just leave a response dangling in the air, saying that he knows so-and-so, and what that person knows, but what he himself truly knows, God only knows.

Jamal doesn't know where he's going to go. First he went to Lebanon, to stay with his in-laws, but they grew tired of having him around. He's extremely fat, he just sits at the table eating and smoking like a glutton, talking about his journey to Lebanon and then on to Turkey. You might call him a refugee, though. And then there was Abd al-Qadir, the Bedouin philosophy teacher who fled his house in the Al-Rashideen neighborhood. He moved his wife and two daughters to Reyhanli, then traveled to Mersin, Greece, and Albania, where he was detained for a month before being deported to Greece, where he is still awaiting sentence.

Nader also fled to Mersin, then to Greece, where he tried going to the airport eleven times, but each and every time they seized him in the terminal or on the plane before take-off. And Zakaraya, the other philosophy teacher, joined up with Mahmoud, and the two of them set out for Europe, now they are in Brussels learning the language and wasting their days as they await release from a detention facility.

Saeed, who left for Lebanon, Turkey, Greece, and then Denmark, is learning Danish and how to quit smoking, but why? Because the refugee stipend he receives isn't enough to cover the cost of his habit. They turned his house on Zahraa Street into a sniper's den, installing a small group of fighters, a small window the size of a heart, and a sniper's rifle with which they could strike enemy forces.

People here were no longer afraid. Let's say, for example, that there was an explosion, like there was on Friday, near the Faculty of Engineering, and a rocket landed on some building, making a crater in the foundation. It was as if nothing whatsoever had happened, everyone went to prayer and listened to the imam's sermon, which discussed the woman who went to hell for failing to feed a hungry cat, for not helping it in any way. The imam spoke about the tortures of hell experienced by this woman, horrifying the worshippers. They all filed out of the mosque to go buy vegetables and fruit in the culvert, the same place they would buy dairy products, and then returned to their homes overjoyed by the bounty God had bestowed upon them.

Dump trucks were hauling away debris that bounced around inside the vehicles, a totally unremarkable occurrence, ten, twenty, God only knows how many of them there were. Security forces had cordoned off the spot and were not allowing even a glimpse of what had happened where the rocket had exploded.

When three missiles blew up here in the al-Jumayliyah neighborhood, everyone scattered for a few moments, but they reemerged and cleaned up the glass and everything else that had been broken, taxis took the wounded to the hospital, and then everyone went back about their business as if nothing had happened.

Those of us sitting in the cafe weren't interested in any of that, mostly we were more concerned with matters that affected us directly, like today, for example, I asked Muhammad D (there are so many Muhammads we have to place a special marker beside their names to distinguish one from the others) if he had watched the film *Take Me and My Shame* and he replied that he had seen *Palace Walk* once at the Granada Cinema. I told him that was the second release, and that the first run had been at the Fuad Cinema. You see, you don't know a thing about cinema, I told him, and he objected, proceeding to defend himself by saying he had seen this film and that film, at the fanciest cinema houses. I asked him if he even knew where the Farouq Theater was located. He remained silent. Then the painter chimed in, which proved that he had been eavesdropping on our conversation the whole time, to say that it was located on Bustan Kull Ab Street, and that anyone who went inside feeling good would come out devastated.

The interior section of the table was involved in this conversation, while the outer section was discussing the plight of migrants to Europe. I got involved in that conversation.

"If you say that the birth rate in France is zero," Muhammad D interjected, "then they need fresh blood all over Europe in order to maintain their societies. Doctor Ihab said that is a very high estimate, that French society is in the midst of a serious contraction. Haven't you all heard the expression 'the aging continent'? They need young children there so that they can raise them to be productive workers in their own society."

"But they grow up and all they learn is to buy and sell drugs," said the painter, "and the whole society winds up strung out."

Nobody paid attention to the artist. I decided I would go to the checkpoint in secret, well, anyway I didn't tell anyone about it. I said goodbye to everyone, paid for my coffee, and headed toward the Al-Mamoon secondary school. People were lined up in rows, many carrying empty bags under their arms while some had full bags and wheelbarrows as they approached the checkpoint. I pressed on deeper into the neighborhood between the main drag and the Al-Hikma secondary school, which had been a zone of car repair shops before that moved to Al-Ramouseh, and then I walked down toward the checkpoint.

THE CHECKPOINT: WHAT DO YOU KNOW ABOUT A CHECKPOINT?

The checkpoint is located between two or three vehicles, the first stretches out as wide as the street itself, a run-down government bus, and the other two are more or less the same. There is a broad boulevard between them, a school on the right-hand side and commercial buildings with shops along the left-hand side. Lots of merchants are active around there, some who have come from the villages and others from impoverished neighborhoods. All have brought vegetables to sell, piling them up along the entire length of the street. The other two buses have been stacked one on top of the other, also in the middle of the road to block traffic, along with sandbags tossed helter-skelter to ensure the orderly, single-lane flow of people.

I bought everything I was going to need for that day, then walked toward the bakery for bread, the first time in a long while that I had been able to buy it warm. Standing in line, I struck up a conversation with some of the people around me. I had to wait nearly half an hour for my turn. When I was able to buy three bags, I felt a kind of joy wash over me for the simple fact that I had been able to procure warm bread so easily.

When I got back with just about everything that I had gone out to buy, I was greeted by sniper fire, and as I got closer to home the sounds became noticeably louder. But I still needed zucchini before I would be able to cross everything off my list. I stopped next to a young man in the middle of the street, sitting behind a mound of high-quality zucchini, which is why I chose him, and I proceeded to inspect the produce for the best ones despite the persistent gunfire.

As the shooting intensified, I paid for the squash and rushed over to join some other people taking shelter together. All along the street I saw splotches of blood, more like droplets really, splattered all over, about the size of a gun barrel, and other stains that led directly to the spot where we had all congregated. People were huddled together in building entryways on both sides of the street, fear written all over their faces, and all over mine, too, I'm sure.

The street in front of the school was totally deserted, the sniper's bullets had the place to themselves. Some people who had piled into the building lobbies and were now plastered against the walls had begun to recite Quranic verses like Al-Qassar, Al-Ahadeeth, and Al-Aqwal, each of which expresses the mood of just this kind of situation perfectly. By the time the blood had started to dry, a twenty-something man had invited us all to pray with him, and many obliged.

"The important thing, my friends," the young man said, "is that we all get home in one piece."

Indistinct words were muttered in response.

The collective fear lasted nearly three hours, and a young woman passed around water to everyone who had sat down in the doorway just beside me.

"The sniper shot him in the head, he was just selling vegetables right there," one man said, pointing out the splotch of blood.

"Are we killing each other over tomatoes and cucumbers? Can you see us, Lord?" an old man bellowed.

There was a long silence heavy with fear and sadness. At this point those in front started marching slowly, then gradually accelerating. The road was open and the sniper fire was drawing to an end.

All of a sudden people started pouring out from all directions, packing the area, all of them running toward the Bustan Al-Qasr checkpoint.

After passing through the checkpoint I waited in the Al-Fayd neighborhood for a shared taxi. The communal van I was accustomed to taking wouldn't come through this neighborhood. The driver let out passengers and brought on others from over there. I waited so long that it was starting to seem pointless, but just then I heard a car horn that made me jump, and I pulled myself together as I clung to the vegetables and other items I had bought, and the honking gradually filled the space, piercing my nerves and pulverizing my senses.

"Now they're using even more bullets," I said as I climbed on board.

I watched the shared taxis passing by, all bursting with

passengers, until a police motorcycle, which it turned out was the vehicle making that infernal racket, pulled up beside me.

"Give me your ID," the officer spat out in a way that startled me.

"I don't have it on me," I replied.

"What the . . . ?" he said, as if something had caught in his throat.

"I don't have my ID with me right now," I repeated. "And why would I give it to you anyway?"

"Aren't you the one who just said, 'Even more bullets to boot'?"

"No, I didn't say that."

"I can bring a dozen people who just witnessed you saying that to me."

"No, I never said that."

"Come with me, please."

"I take refuge in God from the accursed Devil."

"You seek refuge from Satan, huh? Well, you've just met him."

"Brother," I said. "I never cursed you, you're not the Devil. Where do you want to take me anyway?"

"Down to the police station so we can come to an understanding with one another."

"What a day, brother. Even if I did say an unkind word, it was to the motorcycle, certainly not to you."

"Well who do you think did the honking?"

"The insult was directed at the sound of the horn. I apologize profusely if you misunderstood."

"There's no need to apologize. Personally, I'd prefer that you come along with me on your own recognizance, otherwise . . ."

"And what about all this stuff I'm carrying," I said, gesturing toward the vegetables and other groceries.

"You can leave them right there. I don't think you're going to need them anymore."

I turned the whole thing over in my mind. This policeman wasn't about to let me reach the shores of safety unless I went along with him, but they were just going to paint me as a terrorist, claim I was wearing an explosive vest or something, that I was trying to blow myself up near them, that they had arrested me before I could carry out my suicide bombing. I put down what I was carrying, reached my hand into my pocket, and pulled out two hundred liras that I pressed into the policeman's hand.

"All good now?"

"All good now," he said, taking the money. "Don't let this happen again."

He sped away, his horn blaring as people cleared out of his way, everyone silent, including me.

MY SON, WITHOUT ANY PROTECTION

I barely had time to put down the groceries and say hello to my wife before there was a knock at the door. I hurried over to open it and found Muhammad A, my son's friend from medical school, standing there. It was strange for him to show up without my son.

"Please come in, Muhammad," I said. "You're most welcome."

"I'm sorry, uncle," he said from his very tall height. "It's Nawwar, I don't know how to tell you this."

"What is it? Has something happened to him?"

He started to turn pale and then blurted out, "Nawwar's fine." I remained silent as Muhammad A continued. "He's been detained . . . security agents raided the university. There was a conference. They arrested him while he was just sitting there taking notes." After saying this he turned around and darted toward the staircase.

I looked back at my wife to find her nearly collapsed, so I grabbed hold of her and helped her inside. The two of us sat there in shock. Because he was an only son, he had been exempted from military service, and she spoiled him as if he were an only child. We had just one son and one daughter. My daughter holds a doctorate in engineering. I'm an Arabic language schoolteacher. I go off to my work every morning and return afterward to the Island Cafe, where I sit for two hours or so and then go shopping for fruits and vegetables and other groceries we need for the house. That's how things used to be anyway, but now with the siege of the city, the only thing ahead of me is the checkpoint.

Now my son is being held in state security prison: what am I supposed to do? His mother casts me a meaningful glance, as if to suggest that I'm the one who detained him, who threw him into my own personal jail with the state security. She didn't say a word at first, just glared at me.

Then she let loose, saying I was to blame for what happened to her son.

"Good grief, woman, pull yourself together. What have I got to do with what they've done to him?"

When our daughter got home and we informed her what had happened, she just sat there in silence, in a moment of total oblivion, and then my wife got up to change her clothes.

"Where are you going?" I asked.

"To the security station," she said.

"I'm going with you," my daughter chimed in. "At least we can bring him some lunch, a blanket, and some warm clothes."

"And a bed and bedding."

"What are you talking about?" my wife asked.

"Nothing," I said. "Nothing at all."

We agreed that my wife and daughter would go, and that I would stay home and feed the chickens. We didn't actually have any chickens or anyone for me to grieve with at all. My wife had said that purely out of spiteful sarcasm. The two of them grabbed those things and left. I expressed my wish that they would be back soon with Nawwar because there was no way he could have done anything against the government. They loaded everything into the car and took off.

Nawwar was a very respectful boy, and before he got arrested, he was a fourth-year medical student. For a while he had participated in the demonstrations, chanting with his friends in the public squares and at the mosques for the fall of the regime, and the regime nearly did fall, otherwise he definitely would have already been arrested, which is to say, if armed people hadn't gotten involved, and when those armed people first got involved in the revolution, he said the revolution had failed. He gave up on it altogether and focused entirely on his studies.

He was once held for a week by the criminal police. He had gone to the Al-Hariri neighborhood because there was going to be a demonstration there, but by the time he arrived it was already finished, and they were confronted instead with police who had congregated there. They wrote up a report claiming he had been arrested on suspicion of involvement in some crimes: arson of public buildings, assault with a deadly weapon, and fomenting sectarian hatred.

It was Ramadan, the month of fasting to mark when the Quran had been revealed to the Prophet Muhammad.

My wife and daughter started delivering Nawwar two grilled chickens, along with pickled vegetables and garlic sauce, two loaves of bread spread with hot pepper paste; they'd also bring him a blanket, fresh underwear, and plastic flip-flops.

Our son was sentenced to one week in prison, accused of taking part in a demonstration, and they later released him in accordance with the promulgation of an amnesty for all who had committed bloodless crimes. After he got out, we asked him about the underwear, but he said he never got it. Then we asked him about the chicken, and he said they used to give him one wing every day, which led us to conclude that they would not provide him with any protection.

That was the first time, and now it's the second time, but that was the police, while this is state security. What's the difference, though, I thought to myself.

When my wife and daughter got back, I asked how their visit to state security went. My wife wouldn't respond but my daughter told me they weren't able to see him. "They told us they'd deliver him all the stuff we brought."

Then I asked if they'd found out why he was arrested in the first place, and she said, "Apparently he's wanted in Damascus."

My wife started moving back and forth, venom dripping from her all the while. Whenever I asked her a question, she'd walk away. Now I just let her go and dropped my head in my hands. "May God release us from this burden and free him from prison."

"What are you saying?" my wife asked.

"Nothing," I replied. "Nothing at all."

The time our son spent languishing in prison dragged on, and, according to our understanding of what was happening, he had been transferred to Damascus for questioning. We went to see them the very next day, and they told us something or other . . . and so we kept on kissing the hands of those who might be able to do something for us as well as those who couldn't, speaking with some person who I wouldn't even buy an onion skin from and then another who had been elected a member of parliament and who would help people in circumstances like this one. I went to see him, kissed his hand, and prayed for his good fortune, though as the Syrian saying goes, nothing came of that prayer but cumin. I've never been sure exactly what that phrase is supposed to mean but somehow it still seemed perfectly apt to our situation. And then there was the writer whose reputation spread all across the country for participating in the revision of the constitution; we also went to his house to see him, where he told us he couldn't really do anything to help. We paid a visit to the head of the Arab Writers' Union as well, who was also a member of parliament, and this man did what he said he would, going to visit our son at state security, but he couldn't do much of anything helpful in the end either. We visited and visited but nobody was able to get anything done for us. The responses we received were all the same: there was no record of anyone by that name.

My wife would wake up in the middle of the night screaming, weeping until her voice rose up into the seven heavens, only the sky would remain closed and as her voice reverberated its way back down to her she would shove it aside and send it to hell. In the end, nobody could hear her cries, and she told me our son was gone for good. If I told her that patience was the key to salvation, she'd explode into screaming and wailing. What was I supposed to do? On the one hand, my son was stuck in jail, while on the other, I had to contend with his mother and her infernal voice. Soon I was walking in a perpetual daze, she'd be talking to me from the east and I'd reply to her in the west, sometimes I wouldn't even respond at all. The folks at the cafe who knew about my situation would say, hang in there, everything's going to be fine. I never knew what to say in return.

On the tenth day we got a phone call from a human rights organization. I gave them all the information they asked for so they could look into the matter.

On the thirty-first day we got a phone call from someone who told us he was a friend of our son's from prison, who said, "Don't worry, Nawwar is fine, he's alive and well, and he's being held at the general Mukhabarat prison in Kafr Sousseh. He's in Damascus."

This calmed us down a bit. On the thirty-ninth day we received more news over the telephone from another friend of his from Deraa, informing us that he was still alive.

Things became more dramatic in the following days. Every day Nawwar's mother went to the state security station waiting for them to accept the underwear she brought with her, that's all she wanted from them, to let him change his clothes because she simply couldn't take it anymore. She went to speak with the Party bureau administration on the university campus, explaining to them how her son had been taken away while taking notes at a conference, that he had done nothing wrong, and how he was a patriotic citizen. A party representative at the university told her that he sympathized with her plight but that there was nothing he could do. Then she paid a visit to the medical school where he was studying, and they told her the exact same thing. All we could do was wait.

It had been several days of waiting when I got a phone call from the military police in Aleppo explaining that our son was with them, that we should try not to worry, and that he was going to be released the next day. I allowed myself to feel some excitement but I squelched that feeling as I informed my wife that we had found him, that the next day he would be home with us, God willing. My wife cast me a dubious glance and silently marched into the other room.

It took all of the strength I had to endure the waiting for the next day, to keep my nerves together. I couldn't sleep all night—I was plagued by images of a ravenous bug hunting for its prey. My head wouldn't stop pounding even after I had popped a few Paracetamols and swallowed my blood pressure medication. I was still in pain, and around 4:00 a.m. it got so bad I jumped out of bed and went to the bathroom to wash my face. Without drying off, I sat back down on the edge of the bed, like someone dangling at the edge of an abyss, and I remained there until the first threads of light began to divide from the blackness all around me, then I lay back down on the bed and slept for a bit, dreaming about a hyena as it devoured my body. I was screaming, and had a hard time waking up. There was nothing there but me and the bed.

My wife had gotten dressed and was standing by the door. She didn't say good morning, didn't speak a word, just glared at me.

"Everything okay?" I asked, as I gradually found my bearings.

"Well, are we going to see him or what?"

I told her it was 7:15 a.m., they don't open until 8:00, and they probably wouldn't even bring him out before 11:00.

"I'm going to see my son. You can stay here if you want."

"God grant me patience, hang on while I throw some clothes on."

I got dressed in a hurry and walked out as she had already started to leave.

They transported him from the military police to the Ministry of Justice, where they were going to hand him over to the prison police. What a nightmare, I swear to God.

We waited there at the Justice Ministry until 1:00 p.m., when some good tidings of hope started to emerge. They hauled out criminals and thieves and people with long rap sheets, and my son Nawwar came along with them. After forty-five days we were finally able to see him. We walked inside the Justice Ministry prison. My wife had made arrangements with the warden, who allowed us to see him. We handed him some fresh underwear and he changed on the spot. His beard had grown long and thick. I nearly broke down in tears at the sight of him. Meanwhile his mother was already crying. The reunion lasted until 2:00 p.m., which is when they asked us to leave. And so we waited . . . fifteen minutes, half an hour, an hour, but still they didn't call his name. Then they loaded up all the prisoners in a windowless prison van and took them away, shutting down the Justice Ministry prison, and shuffling us all outside. When my wife learned that our son was not going to be tried that day, and that she'd have to wait another day before seeing him, she started to howl, a cry that became more intense when the door shut us out. The police had to escort her out by force as the presiding judge Hussein Farho slipped out to his car through the side door. I tried to help her walk but she declined my assistance, grabbing hold of the metal door and refusing to leave. She was crying and sobbing, cursing and insulting and squealing. She remained like this for nearly half an hour, until the police began to feel some pity for her, until the sky started to cry on her.

I held onto her so that she wouldn't fall down, hailed a cab, shoved her inside, and laid her down in bed when we got home, where she didn't move a muscle.

The next day my son arrived early in a prison van. I paid off the police to let me ride with them, and we drove to see the judge who had released him under the amnesty for those who had committed bloodless crimes. I was able to go along with the police because I had showered them with money as my son smudged a fingerprint here and added a signature there before he was released. And then, finally, there we were with our son, his hands free, outside the Justice Ministry. After bribing the police who were trailing us, we made our way home.

My son told us how they had come for him while he was taking notes, which we already knew, insisting that he hadn't done anything wrong, reinforcing the lawsuit we had already filed in his case, now being raised in Damascus. They had whisked away my son to Damascus for further interrogation, he was flown from the state security station to the capital, where they welcomed him with beatings, torturing some parts of his body but leaving him untouched elsewhere. The beatings continued every day until the evening, when they would let up. He had endured forty-five days of this, the duration of his prison time, and they released him after the amnesty law was promulgated, taking him to Homs and then to Aleppo, first to the military police, then the city jail, and finally to the Justice Ministry.

"Thank God you're home," we said to him, but he didn't reply, meeting us with nothing but silence. Over the course of the next few days Nawwar turned inward and didn't speak to anyone. He stayed in his room, eating and drinking all by himself and refusing to go to university. His studies had gone up in smoke. If we set foot in his room he'd start yelling at us, he didn't want to see anyone except for his mother, who would bring him food, place it on the table, then sit down on the bed beside him, stroking his head and his shoulders, cursing the university and education that had brought him to this, and he nodded his head in agreement. As soon as she left he'd start cursing and swearing, hiding beneath the sheets, and then leave in a hurry. A week went by like this. The boy needed water but we didn't have any to offer him. The water had been shut off and our tanks were dry, so I picked up the plastic jug and went off in search of water. The water had been shut off at the mosque as well even though they had dug a well with donations from the pious. It was almost five in the morning and I was out in search of water when I noticed a young man carrying some. I asked him where he had found it and he pointed me in the right direction. I walked over to where I found just a few men and women waiting in line. I put down the tank and stood there to wait, too. There were only six taps, but all had been shut off, leaving just dribbles. I wondered what I should do and I decided to wait.

It took one of those people a half hour to fill his tank, but the man didn't stop there, pulling out another tank and placing it underneath the impeded tap. I waited another half hour until it had been filled, at which point he took his water and left. Then a woman filled her tank and left. When it was my turn I placed the tank under the broken, leaky spout as the rest of the people in line waited without talking to one another for whatever water remained. The man whose house we were at came out to throw out his garbage. He was wearing a white undershirt and shorts that extended slightly below his knees. After tossing the garbage he went back inside, without a word to us, only an icy stare. My tank was just about full and I was getting ready to leave when the man standing behind me asked, "You only have one tank?" I nodded as I picked it up and headed for home. By the time I opened the door it was 8:30 a.m. I could hear my wife crying so I went to see her after putting down the water. She was sobbing all alone.

"He's gone," she said.

"Who?"

"Nawwar left."

"Where did he go?"

"I don't know, maybe Turkey. There's nothing left for me here. I have to leave."

"And go where?"

"To hell," she exhaled.

My mind drifted elsewhere as I thought about my son who had left, I had no idea where to.

"How can you space out in a moment like this?" my wife asked. "I'm telling you I can't take it here in this country anymore. Find us another place to live."

"I'm still in a bit of a daze," I told her. "Just let me think for a minute."

"What's the use in thinking? I want to get out of here."

"But go where?"

"Raqqa. Didn't you say you know a lot of people there? Rent us a house, any house, we'll just go."

"We'll see. I haven't even had a chance to think now that he's disappeared. Let me get dressed and go look for him."

"He must be gone by now, he crossed the checkpoint at seven, headed for Turkey."

"God knows best. Let's wait until tomorrow, then we'll leave for Raqqa to look for a place to live."

It was a struggle to get water to the house. The mosque was very close but the caretakers wouldn't allow people to get water there. I walked inside after morning prayer; the ablution taps were still dripping a little bit, and the faucet by the toilet was running more quickly. I attached the hose and placed it next to the tank, letting the water flow for twenty minutes until it was full, then I picked up the tank and made my way back home.

The regime had opened a new road to Raqqa and Damascus. After a period of time in which the checkpoint seemed to have been closed for good, the vegetables and fruit and other basic goods had started to reach us via that road.

I had no need to tell her that I was going to Raqqa, that I'd have to be away from them for a few days. My wife could no longer bear to remain in the city, so I would go to Raqqa to see my friend Hamadi Abu al-Issa and rent a house, then bring my wife and daughter with me to live there.

RAQQA...CAPITAL OF THE ISLAMIC STATE

We hopped on a Pullman bus that crept through Al-Safira, then Khanasirah, which people around here pronounce Khanasir, where all you could see were soldiers sipping tea and cooking food. One street cuts through the city, which appears to be expanding to the right and to the left, silent and sorrowful: like an old man who has cloaked himself in a shroud and collapsed. As we continue along, we see storefronts with their doors blown off, houses with windows and entryways, nothing whatsoever indicates that this city was ever inhabited except for the rubble piled between the houses. Washing machines with nothing left but their skeletons, refrigerators tossed here and there have been converted into dining tables, and the early morning is still written all over the soldiers' eyes; they have not yet woken up completely.

Here we are in the center of the Al-Safira neighborhood, where the walls have been painted over and the Al-Safira police, Khanasir division, have written words of welcome to visitors, scrawled in beautiful calligraphy: "We Obey You, Zaynab." The Pullman has to stop at a checkpoint.

"Where are you going?" the soldier asked the driver.

"Hama."

The bus attendant, who happened to be the driver's son, got out of the vehicle, a glass of cold water in his hand. The soldier waved the bus along as he raised the glass of water up high and poured the water into his mouth.

"No to Sectarianism," announces one wall over here, and over there are some more walls with the same words of welcome and praise for the Prophet's granddaughter.

Now we're on the Athriya Road, a narrow route that is just barely wide enough to accommodate two cars, typically it's used as a footpath between villages. The army has taken up positions along the ridges and the heights, and they have also made it down into the lowlands where they have built fortified defense posts, some of them now furnished with creature comforts as well.

We continued on our way through nearly empty countryside. It was autumn, the sky was blue and there wasn't a hint of rain, on a level road where nobody bothered us, and it was serene enough for us to doze off for a bit had it not been for the periodic clattering and rattling of our bus. Larks and other birds soared to and fro all along the asphalt road, flying away in what seemed like glee as the bus approached and alighting on the dirt beyond the road. I closed my eyes for a bit, we still had a long way to go. Now we're on the international highway and in two hours at the most we should be in Raqqa. Nowadays, though, we'd need five or six hours to get there, depending on the checkpoints.

The road had become extremely long, and it was no longer international.

The Athriya Road led us to a large factory where the army had installed itself, to the right lies Salamiyah, then Damascus, and to the left Al-Tabqa, then Raqqa. We encountered several low-slung checkpoints, which forced the bus to proceed in a zigzag so they wouldn't be ambushed by any enemies. Several army soldiers carrying Russian-made rifles boarded the bus, sat down in silence, pulled out some tobacco to roll cigarettes, and then started smoking. We were just eighteen passengers, a fairly small group, including the young son of the driver.

Without attracting any unwanted attention, the bus made its way down the road, which had no turn-offs, as if it had been drawn with a ruler. We rarely saw other cars out there, unlike on the Athriya-Salamiyah Road, which always seems to be clogged with cars and buses as well as vans both with and without passengers.

After a while, we were stopped at an army checkpoint and the bus attendant hurried to hand over a glass of cool water, when they asked, "Where to?"

"Raqqa," the driver replied, and they waved us ahead.

I had visited Raqqa many times before, ever since the eighties, when I was able to go there in the morning, taking the international road, store my belongings wherever I was going to stay, have some food, then hang out by the Euphrates, sit along the banks and watch the river flow past as it was sculled by an old man worn down by time, with a gray beard and a peasant face, prayer beads in his hand as he repeatedly muttered the name of God most high.

The river would captivate me for long stretches of time, as I reminisced about the parties that used to happen there: a group of young men diving into the river, eating fish they had caught themselves, singing, and if the spirit moved them you would see them spring to their feet and start dancing in the Bedouin style, staying up until dawn moving to the beat of the darbuka and the oud and the voice of the singer, who sang about estrangement from the beloved, sorrow, and heartbreak.

The bus slowed to a halt as we approached the next check-point. A man in fatigues came on board, offered his greet-ings, and gave us all a once-over before asking for everyone's ID. After we handed them over, he checked the documents one by one and then inspected the bus, quickly peering in any hidden spaces, shoving his hand inside and rummaging around. He didn't find anything of interest and invited the driver to move along.

In the forty-five years I have been coming to Raqqa, I have never gotten bored of this small, modest city. Many mayors have served here, and all have ignored corruption, to say nothing of those who directly contributed to its spread. Imagine with me, if you will, how the streets were to be paved twice every year, once as it was budgeted officially, once in order to line the pockets of fat cats, and still the streets of Raqqa remained unpaved.

There was nothing different at the third and fourth check-points, everyone followed the exact same routine—asking to see IDs, searching the bus, then saying, "Go in peace." The driver would forge ahead as if he had been scalded by fire. Now we were at the top of Al-Ayman Street. When the bus stops the attendant shouts that we're going to have a ten-minute break, for those who wish to smoke or do something else, have some water or get some food, they are welcome to go ahead and do so.

The rest stop was located on a slight rise that looked out over vast tracts of empty land. We walked up the steps to enter the shop, which sold all kinds of food and drinks, but I wasn't hungry so I went outside to the water fountain, washed my face well, and then headed back toward the bus. There were dozens of empty bottles and packages alongside the vehicle. The other passengers had begun to return, buttoning their pants after urinating standing up on the desolate land. The only ones left to wait for were the soldiers getting on board here.

After the break, the bus had traveled for another half hour when the attendant stood up and gestured toward his face, placing his palm against his nose.

"Cover up, ladies," he said.

The women and girls hurriedly filed to the back of the bus, pulled out their niqabs, and placed them on their heads. I watched two of them in particular, two women I thought were sisters: one was a hairstylist and cosmetologist, and I overheard her explain her work to another woman and offer her phone number. When I first came on board I noticed that she and her sister were both unveiled and had makeup on, which caused me to doubt whether this could truly be the bus to Raqqa.

There were seven women on the bus and now they were all sitting in the rear, niqabs covering their faces. When the bus attendant was satisfied that his request had been honored, he sat back down in his seat as his father lit up a cigarette and started puffing smoke out the window, staring out into the distance with some concern, in a daze. I had no idea what had come over him.

"Welcome to the Islamic State of Iraq and Syria," read the writing on a banner flapping in front of me, and on the massive black flags I saw all around as well. The road was littered with earthen barriers, which the bus traversed before stopping to wait its turn. All of us were silent, wary and more than fearful to be honest. We had to wait for about five minutes until a young man with a long beard appeared beside the driver, wearing a long flowing shirt that reached below his knees, matching pants, annd a pistol hanging from a holster. He had cradled a rifle on his shoulder, grenades cinched to his bandolier, and a walkie talkie in his hand into which he spoke in a Bedouin accent, his flowing hair pulled back behind his head with a handkerchief that was the same color as his clothes, and tattered slippers on his feet.

"As-Salaamu aleikum," he said, and we all replied with the perfunctory *"Wa-aleikum as-salaam."*

"Thank God you have arrived safely," he added, though none of us responded. "Where are you coming from?" From Aleppo, we told him. "Welcome, welcome."

He pulled out a few young men, those who had been conscripted for compulsory military service, at least, those he assumed would have been, asked for their mobile phones to be handed over to him as well, and he carefully examined their ID cards and compared them to their faces, then returned the documents to them, only a few people really, maybe four, and then he continued on to the women, standing beside the head of each one of them and asking who they were traveling with. One of them responded in a whisper. He then asked for the name of their mother and father, and when he was satisfied that everyone was trustworthy, he wished us all a safe and pleasant journey.

A little while after the bus had started moving once again, we all saw the Al-Tabqa military air field, where there seemed to be no movement whatsoever, where you couldn't even smell the presence of human beings, then we made our way past the Al-Tabqa exit, where there were some houses, a decimated gas facility, and a fighter jet that had been placed there for show, also completely destroyed.

We were stopped next at the Al-Tabqa international checkpoint, although nobody boarded the bus this time, they were satisfied with simply asking the driver, "From where?" They waved us through as soon as we told them, and the bus headed for Al-Mansoureh, where we stopped to let off some passengers before speeding off on the home stretch to Raqqa. We only had twenty minutes to go, a half hour at most. I nodded off for a bit. My sleep had been troubled lately, I wasn't able to sleep at all really, and I soon saw the river appear on the left-hand side flooding and irrigating crops, shimmering in the light, its blue color nourishing the earth and turning it green.

Here we are in Raqqa. The road forked into two, one leading to Dayr al-Zur and the other to the Islamic State in Raqqa. The road was shaded by cinchona trees, which blanketed their shadows along the path with a mother's tenderness. Finally we arrived at the checkpoint that would grant us entry to the city.

A young man climbed into the bus, looking no different than the one from the last checkpoint, also covered with weaponry. He greeted us all with a sprightly, smiling face, and we responded enthusiastically while he gathered our identification, then strode over to the women to ask them the same questions—who is your male guardian, who is his mother? The endearing thing about our group was the fact that the woman who worked as a stylist had brought along her twelve-year-old son, establishing him as a guardian for her and her sister.

The bus turned off to the right, toward the bus station. It was 1:15. I grabbed my bag, descended from the bus, and headed out of the station. Drivers were squawking at me, and I hopped into the nicest and newest car I could find, placing the bag in the back seat and sitting down in the passenger seat.

"Mansour Street," I said.

The driver didn't speak to me and I simply stared out at the street. Flying in front of the Cultural Center there was a gigantic black flag announcing the entrance to Raqqa.

"How are things with you all here?" I asked the driver.

"Can't you see?" he said gruffly. "Every Friday they execute some of their critics. We're tired of all the terror, man. Yesterday they murdered three people, right here at the clock tower, and, honestly, people gathered around the monument, so many that I couldn't see a thing."

The traffic police all greeted him warmly but he didn't respond. The officer was wearing the exact same outfit, raising his hand and waving at the cars as people honked at him and drove past. They didn't pay too much attention though, and it appeared he wasn't even carrying a ticket book.

I paid the man my fare and walked into the hotel. By the time I put down my bag, hunger had begun gnawing at me, so I went downstairs to find some food.

Al-Mansour Street, which used to be where ready-to-wear clothing imported from Aleppo was sold, had been transformed entirely by moneychangers, the storefronts now announcing exchange rates with huge images of the Saudi riyal, the American dollar, and the Turkish lira. A few shops had grown into larger operations, where fighters and mujahideen—as some people preferred to call them—would exchange money, loaded up with Syrian liras or other currencies, and you could see them strolling around leisurely, two by two, as they counted up all the cash in their hands.

The smaller shops also advertised that they bought and sold currencies, even this tailor who ordinarily repairs the clothing of locals had put up a sign saying he was a moneychanger as well. Jewelers and goldsmiths were doing the same with their shops.

After buying some food at the edge of the museum, I still needed to find some bread, for man truly does live by bread alone, which is how I found my way to the ancient market, which remained as it had been despite the arrival of modern generators. These shops were selling the same things they had sold for the past quarter century, even longer, and my feet guided me from God knows where straight to the clock tower neighborhood, where I found people gathered around, some snapping photos with their mobile phones. I walked up to the monument to see three human heads carefully arranged on top, one to the east and two facing north, placed on the edge of the clock as people took pictures. On the ground, along the base of the clock, were decapitated corpses.

The schoolchildren from the Al-Rasheed School were pouring out of the main gate, all of them chanting, "Hey! Hey! Hey!" and as soon as they were out the door they sprinted over to the clock tower, each and every one of them toting a schoolbag. When they reached the severed heads, they stood in silence and stared up at this spectacle of the greatest terror imaginable.

I headed off to the left, toward February 23 Street, the afterimages of the three massacred victims dancing before my eyes, until I was overcome with crippling nausea. Just then the muezzin called out, *"Allahu Akbar,"* time for prayer. I wanted to get some bread from the bakery but the stores abruptly closed as people left work to go to the mosque and pray and veiled women dressed in black waited on the sides of the street. I didn't know what to do, a stranger in a city caught unawares by the time for prayer. Besides, I wasn't a pious person anyway. There was nobody left in the street except for me and a few children milling about outside the bakery. I stood there with them until the bakery reopened. The employees were still inside, waiting for prayer to finish. A large car drove past calling out for people to come pray. I hid from it. I don't know how I got myself into this mess! Then a young man came by asking the children why they hadn't gone off to pray.

"We've already gone and come back," they lied.

I walked over to a spot where people were gathering. It seemed like they had all just gotten out of the mosque. I stood there with them. My body wouldn't be able to withstand a single lashing, so forget about seventy of them for failing to show up at prayer.

When the bakery finally reopened, the employees were already hard at work, and I stepped inside to buy five loaves for ten liras apiece, then set off toward the north. There was a massive car blasting religious anthems about the virtues of jihad for keeping believers on the straight path.

I veered left and found that another bakery along with whatever else used to be nearby had been reduced to rubble, flattened by a fighter jet: now there was a man selling chicken instead. I was so tired by this point that I stopped right there, my feet couldn't carry me further. There were sandwiches for sale, too, so I ordered one. A young blond man carrying a rifle strutted over and asked how much. I'm not sure what language he was speaking. The owner informed him that he could buy a wrap for two hundred Syrian liras.

"God bless you," the man said, pulling out two one hundred lira notes even as the sandwich maker wrapped some shawarma in bread for him and loaded it up with condiments, including mayonnaise and pickled vegetables. The man started eating ravenously and in silence.

ISIS men were spread all over Raqqa: black men and blonds, blue-eyed Europeans, Africans, Chechens, Tunisians, Libyans, Moroccans, Australians, and Americans: they all rested machine guns against their shoulders, driving or sauntering over to the international store, where they could call their relatives on an international phone line. There had already been several incidents between these foreigners and the local residents, but I never saw such things myself. For example, when a member of ISIS once caught a citizen smoking a cigarette, he told him to put it out and, when the citizen refused, he threatened him with his machine gun and ordered him to hand over the whole pack or else. When the person refused, this ISIS guy brandished his weapon, aimed, and fired, killing the man. There was quite a commotion. The cousin of this smoker came running over and, as soon as he saw the victim, grabbed the ISIS guy, stripped him of his gun away and opened fire on him. Afterward, he started shooting into the air, causing women to wail. The important thing is that they put a stop to those occurrences, covering up the incident and making it disappear. This ISIS guy happened to be from Raqqa and wasn't a foreigner.

On the way back to the hotel I saw six or seven people, sitting and standing, all with their hands or their legs wrapped up. I thought to myself that this must be a general hospital, and I hurried along to the hotel.

There were eight to ten hours of electricity per day here, the water was shut off during the day but flowed during the evening, and gas was sold at impossibly high prices, three thousand five hundred liras per liter. Meanwhile diesel was sold at the official price of eighty liras per liter. There were hundreds of gas stations here, and they all advertised the price per liter of diesel or petroleum or gas, with the sum written on the caps atop the barrels.

When I made it back to my hotel room, I switched on the lights. In Aleppo we were denied the pleasure of electricity, although we paid taxes to the government for it. We all bought amperage meters and electrical generators but that wasn't enough. The government electricity was mostly worthless, and when it did come on we could do the washing and wash ourselves, use the refrigerator and the freezer. All the appliances would come on at once.

As I was preparing my food, a violent explosion rocked the neighborhood.

I heard people shouting about how a regime fighter jet had destroyed an entire building. If the bombing had come from an airplane, I thought to myself, there would no doubt be another strike. Before I could even assess the damage to the hotel room, the plane came back around for another sortie, making the entire building quake, filling the room with dust.

I went to throw open the door and the windows but there were no windows left: the glass had shattered and the balcony doors had been torn off. I looked down at the entrance. All of the guests were sprinting inside to find a place to hide. Some of the wounded were being helped along by their shoulders, blood dripping from their heads, while others had to be carried. Dust continued filling the space as I ran down to the street. Everyone was hiding in concealed entryways. I struggled to find out where the airstrike had taken place but couldn't find it before people started warning that the plane was coming back around for another pass and everyone took shelter inside. The dust started to crust over by the time I was sheltering along with them. I walked to a corner opposite the Al-Salaam Hospital. The result of all this was plain to see: an entire six-story building located beside the hospital had been flattened, there was nothing left standing except for the stores on the ground level, emptied of all their goods. It seemed that the pilot had misfired and hit this building instead of the hospital, or perhaps he had received faulty information from the security services and, though he meant to hit the hospital, aimed for this structure instead.

The shops at the front of the building had been eviscerated, and the Al-Bitar clothing store as well as the cars that had been parked out front were ruined. You might say that the shops had all been barbecued and the primary school next door had been destroyed; whatever had been left intact was brought outside. There were stores beyond the immediate blast zone that had been damaged, all the way down to the pharmacy, and to the square that is off to the side of the explosion, to the left, right, and in front of which there was nothing but remains brought into the street. You could see fans that used to hang inside, goods that could no longer be sold in stores. The street where I was staying hadn't sustained too much damage, just some shattered glass here and there.

It was an awful day. I went back to my hotel room to try and pull myself together. I still hadn't eaten anything. I stretched out on the bed and stared up at the ceiling, unable to tell whether I was asleep or awake.

In the evening I went outside to walk around and buy more groceries. As soon as I stepped into the street, I saw militiamen shouting at people and at cars passing by, insulting them and ordering them to keep away from the blast site. I leaned over so that I could see the building where the two missiles had landed, and there were workers who had climbed up to the level above the storefronts clearing away debris, slow and dangerous work. As spotlights shone on the rubble, an armed human wall took shape, a battalion of the Islamic State had occupied the place. The general hospital had to be shut down, the Al-Salaam Hospital had already been closed for a while. Tunisians, Libyans, and Moroccans were cursing at everyone, trying to push them away. Shopkeepers were picking up glass and pulling out doors, air conditioners, and scattered products, sweeping everything out of the stores as some passersby watched and others ran away. I walked right past without paying attention to anything going on.

I didn't have to walk far until Raqqa became the city

I liked, the city I remembered. A grilled meat vendor had begun to set up, placing tomatoes and spicy red pepper and other vegetables in front of him, the chopped parsley mixed with diced onions to make the biyaz salad. His lowly assistant was lighting up the fire, shouting at the top of his lungs, "Get your food here!" spraying down the cucumber and tomato to wash them. If you walked a bit further on you'd find a few shops on February 23 Street that sold just about anything. Here was a clay-oven bakery that displayed its bread outside the storefront with only two people working inside, one selling and one handling the oven: the loaves went in and then came out piping hot with a delicious aroma. If we walked a little bit more we would find a more affordable bakery, where people had come from all over to form a long line that stretched all the way to the end of the street and even wrapped around to the next block. Women stood here waiting their turn, all of them wrapped up tight in their clothes, nothing visible but their eyes, which they had beautifully lined with kohl, their eyelashes sticking straight out and announcing a hidden beauty, but the Islamic State men were too busy shopping for clothes and other things to notice, you'd find them in the shop that looked out on the main square, the one that sold camouflage gear and shirts that extended down below the knees, available in the colors of the desert or the colors of trees, under which they wore camouflage pants that came to the ankle, and then holsters to carry their pistols, and bandoliers that wrapped across their chests with niches to hold grenades and guns, head coverings and sandals. There were products of every make and color, for civilian life and for combat. There were three or four of them inside with the merchant, trying things on as the owner told them, "Mashallah, my friend, it fits you perfectly." Meanwhile another guy stared into the mirror and tried to hold back his smile as he asked about the price. "Just take it, my friend," the merchant replied. "You're a mujahid in the path of God against the infidels, you deserve even more than this." But the mujahid didn't know any Arabic, although he sensed that the owner was paying him a compliment. He grabbed his companion by the chin and pulled him over, asking him to translate how much the owner had asked for, which was three thousand. The mujahid reached into his pocket and pulled out a wad of cash and handed it to the man he had brought over, who counted it for the owner and then purchased a holster in which he could place his pistol that he was going to use to kill infidels. The owner wrapped up what the man had purchased and said goodbye to him at the door, then returned to the two men who were still in the shop so that he could begin working with them on another sale.

Islamic State fighters never quibbled about prices. This is the price, so here, no matter how much the item they were buying may have cost.

I crossed the small plaza over toward the public park, which I reached just as the sun was going down. The shadows made the place a little chilly. I sat down on a bench, recovering from the exhaustion I felt from the hot sun that was saying goodbye to another day. I stood up to wash my face and feet in the nearby fountain and patted my hands dry, then returned to the same seat to relax for fifteen minutes or so. I strolled around the park for a bit. There were two ISIS guys with wives and children to the right of the entrance whom I avoided as I continued north on my way out of the park. There was a monument that had been demolished and thrown to the ground. Here was a hand, there was the head, that was a leg, and here was the rest of the body. The place was littered with the remnants of this monument. I turned left along the border of the park, walked along the outside, and it appeared that the Al-Shuhada Church had been converted into an Islamic Affairs Bureau, as far as I could tell, there were two men with long hair and unkempt beards dressed in ISIS clothes standing in front of the large door. The organization had also seized control of the party bureaus and all of the security services, transforming them into their own offices after painting them yellow, which I noticed when I first arrived in Raqqa. They built fences around large tracts of land they had seized, writing in large letters, "Property of the Islamic State."

Walking back from the market I saw the same thing. I decided not to return to gawk at the Clock Square, so I headed back into the market. Everything was exactly the way it had been the last time I visited Raqqa. The price of vegetables and other goods was much cheaper than in Aleppo. Here the prices were reasonable. Also, there was no theft here because a thief would risk having his hand chopped off, and there was no adultery or homosexuality in this city. I felt strange in the market buying supplies. Here I am coming back by way of Al-Mansour Street, beginning in the museum district, rising up to the main street. An ISIS man stared at me as two of them changed money back into Syrian liras. One of them just stood there gawping at me for a long time as I stumbled past. What did this man want from me? I looked back at him as he sized me up, then reached his hand out toward me, stretching out his finger. I felt my skin turning pale. His friend spoke French with him and smiled. Then he asked, "Aren't you so-and-so?"

Does this man know me? I wondered. What's his deal?

"Yes, I'm so-and-so. Can I help you?"

A FRENCH FILMMAKER IN EGYPT

When I visited Paris, he was the only one waiting for me outside the airport, holding a sign with my name on it, and when he saw me smile he lowered the sign and motioned for me to approach him. As I drew closer, he introduced himself.

"I'm Abd al-Qadir's friend. He couldn't get out of work so I came in his place to take you to him."

"Nice to meet you, but he promised me he was going to pick me up at the airport."

"I know, that's why he sent me."

He was an olive-skinned young man, his thick hair pulled back, like a Hollywood celebrity, wearing pants, a long-sleeved shirt, a sport coat, and brown loafers, with a neatly trimmed mustache and beard.

"This way, please," he said, and I followed him. I had only one piece of luggage, which he picked up and carried for me. I noticed he was wearing a gold ring on one finger.

He guided me to the airport taxi stand where there was a line of black Peugeots waiting their turn. After stowing my suitcase in the trunk he gestured for me to hop into the first car in line, so I climbed into the back seat. He addressed the driver in French and the Peugeot took off. It was a little before five as we left Orly.

"Sir," he said, turning toward me and speaking in Arabic now, "women here are plucked and gobbled up like peeled and seedless grapes."

"Well, back home your own parents managed to create you," I said, nodding at him. "Wouldn't you say your father must have had his share of that same fruit?"

As the Peugeot drove into the city, I was nearly struck dumb. The Paris you see on TV is nothing like the Paris I was seeing before my eyes, it's more beautiful, more splendid, more amazing. No sooner had we arrived at the street where Abd al-Qadir lives than I heard his voice calling down to me from the fourth floor. I looked up to see Abd al-Qadir in the flesh. It had been twenty-one years since I saw him last. He was working for Euro News. He came downstairs and in the blink of an eye he was right in front of me, while Bahaa settled up with the taxi driver, grabbing my suitcase because I was too busy greeting my old friend, the one called Abd al-Qadir. The whole time we climbed the four flights of the staircase, slowly rising toward the sky, Abd al-Qadir was the only one who spoke.

I left behind all my troubles, all my worries. In the evening I cleansed myself of all the filth, washed my body well. Then we had a dinner that Abd al-Qadir had prepared in my honor before leaving the house to truly begin my visit to Paris. That night we wound up somewhere that Abd al-Qadir had selected especially for me, a place where women with the most beautiful voices sang, in French, *bien sûr*. Bahaa was always by our side. Abd al-Qadir took a break from work to show me the real Paris. The next day we strolled down the Champs-Élysées and I was flabbergasted, convinced that I was dreaming but couldn't wake up. We went to Montmartre, the Bibliothèque Nationale and the Musée National, a Picasso exhibition, the Latin Quarter and the Cité Universitaire, Versailles, Père Lachaise: no stone was left unturned. The truth was that Bahaa and Abd al-Qadir were more than just noble men, more than just friends, more than just brothers—they were all of that combined, and then some.

We were sipping coffee in the sun at a cafe on the Champs-Élysées where Jean-Paul Sartre, father of existentialism, used to sit, when I asked Bahaa what he did for a living.

"I'm a film director," he said.

Abd al-Qadir guffawed violently, which I found quite odd. He told me he had never graduated from film school.

"Listen here, my friend," said Abd al-Qadir. "Bahaa used to be married, and he went to film school regularly."

"So what happened?" I asked.

"His wife was very wealthy and she was unfaithful to him. One time he convinced her to travel to Egypt. *Umm al-Dunya*, Mother of the World, they call the place, isn't that right, bey? He was going to pretend to be a famous French filmmaker. Anyway, Bahaa travelled to Egypt with his wife, they stayed at the Gezira Sheraton, announcing that he was a French filmmaker who had come to Egypt to make a movie. All kinds of actors and actresses came to see him, Egyptian filmmakers, too, anyone who had any connection to the film industry. Eventually he made the acquaintance of a woman with Swiss citizenship staying at the same hotel, and he cultivated a relationship with her. Long story short, it developed to the point that his wife realized he was being unfaithful to her, and she accused him outright of doing so, and then one day his wife packed her bags, bound for Paris, and left Bahaa at the hotel without any money. He couldn't even pay the hotel bill. Anyway, he managed to sort things out for himself and return to Paris, because when the Swiss lady found out what was going on she gave him the boot as well. When he arrived back here, he went home to find that his wife had changed the locks and she invited me over to pick up everything that belonged to him, from clothes to cologne. She didn't let me inside the house, though, just chucked everything out the window when she spotted him waiting downstairs."

We all had a laugh about it, then Abd al-Qadir continued, "When he came back, he quit film school, left cinema behind, no longer aspiring to be a director. He's been looking for work ever since. He's not really qualified to do anything, though. He's tried applying to a modeling agency, searching from company to company, sending out his resume and qualifications. If you ask me his appearance and his clothes make him seem like a mannequin, and he'd love to work for Yves Saint Laurent or Chanel or something like that, but they all agree that he's about five centimeters too short."

Bahaa was of Lebanese descent and his mellifluous voice betrayed a Beiruti accent.

"Brother," he said, "I'm from the Aicha Bakkar neighborhood of Beirut, my family fled to Germany when I was one year old. I grew up there, learned German, and my mother died when I was ten, she died giving birth to my brother Barhoum. My father got married to another Lebanese woman there, and as soon I turned eighteen I moved here to Paris. This is the capital of beauty and refinement. I hung out in cafe after cafe until I met the woman who became my wife."

"Tell him how much older than you she is," Abd al-Qadir interjected.

"Her age doesn't matter," he said, ignoring his comment. "So I enrolled at the film academy, travelled to Egypt with her, then I met Abd al-Qadir. He's such a good friend."

He went on to speak at length about Abd al-Qadir, enumerating his virtues. Abd al-Qadir got up to make coffee for us, and Bahaa continued, "Don't believe a word he says. It's all lies. Lies, I tell you!"

"But how can I not believe him when Abd al-Qadir's sitting right here, when I'm in his house? I know him too well. He's my old friend from Aleppo. We used to sit in cafes there every day, too, until he got a university scholarship and came here to study. I stayed back home teaching schoolchildren: subject, object, predicate, verbs, and the neuter form."

At this point I remembered the unusual thing that Bahaa had said to me. I turned toward him. We had all become quite comfortable with one another by this point, so I said, "Bahaa, you told me that women here are gobbled up like grapes! But I didn't see a single woman who even noticed you! Brother, nobody wants to be compared to grapes, even if they are tasty."

Abd al-Qadir overheard our conversation and he came in with two cups of coffee, laughing. "You mean to say you understood that women will just go with anyone who knows how to peel them?"

"Yes," I replied.

ABU MUHAMMAD AND
BAHAA AL-DIN AL-FARANSI

This is Bahaa, whose name had been changed to Abu Muhammad Bahaa al-Din al-Faransi, whom I met in Raqqa, capital of the Islamic State in Iraq and Syria. He hadn't forgotten about our friendship that lasted for a month back when I was in Paris visiting my friend Abd al-Qadir. I had a great time with the two of them experiencing Paris, City of Lights, as they call it.

The man welcomed me in Raqqa, invited me to come and see him, so we made a plan to meet at the Al-Amasi restaurant, located across from the Al-Rashid cafe, near the clock tower, at 8:30. I wondered whether that was a good idea as I searched for my friend Hamadi Abu al-Issa. We had said goodbye to one another, planning to meet again in the evening at the restaurant.

First I wandered off to the right, the side of the square where the bakery is located. People were in two lines that extended all the way back into the square, wrapping around the street on the other side, waiting their turn just to buy some bread. An Islamic State militiaman watched over one line that was specified for women in niqabs, who chattered with one another about their daily lives through their veils. Even if you were only trying to get two loaves of bread you still had to stand in line. Everyone is the same, it makes no difference whether you're a man or a woman, young or old, it doesn't make a difference how pious you might be. The bakery that had been obliterated used to be on the opposite side of the square. People say that a meteor that fell from the sky had pulverized it, resulting in the death of dozens of people. I turned right onto Al-Wadi Street, trying to piece together my fragmentary knowledge of the streets and buildings of Raqqa just in case I made it to Hamadi's house but couldn't find him there. I knew what his building looks like, I had slept there before, that day I had gone to Raqqa with Abu Mahmoud, my friend whose side I never left. We had been invited for a night out on the Euphrates, having called up and rallied seven people to meet up with us. We gathered by the river and found a place off to the side, or I should say they found a spot for us out of the way. They had sent two people ahead of us to lay out a picnic with blankets, bringing a barbecue and coal and skewers, a fan for cooking and utensils. Two other people went to get vegetables and fruit, another two went to buy meat, and the last one came to pick us up at the bus station.

Hamadi Abu al-Issa picked us up in his Kia, then drove to park in front of the snack vendor, where he bought some stuff before we headed toward the Euphrates. At night the river looked like an old man dressed in white, as if the moon were looking down at him and laughing.

Once everyone had come together the party started. A musician showed up with his oud, which he started strumming as he belted out some songs. We were quite a group of young men, some grilling meat on skewers, some making salad, and others just sitting there and smoking, observing the oud player. The great river was beside us, listening in.

Now the performer was really ready. A tabla player had taken up his place, and the concert was about to begin. Without warning the performer began serenading the Euphrates, singing about forbidden lovers as they secretly embrace one another, and about separation. Some of us smoked cigarettes, we poured out arak, which we mixed with water and ice cubes. "Come on, everyone," someone called out to the crowd as the food was cooked directly on the grill. At first we had mezzehs to go with our drinks. We drank so much that some of us mistook roosters for donkeys. We ate too much fruit, snacked on too many salty treats. When we heard the sound of the call to dawn prayer ring out, we lethargically made our way toward the river and then dove in after stripping down to our skivvies, plunging into the water and swimming, horsing around with one another, and then getting out when our bodies became too cold. They gave us blankets to wrap ourselves in, but I was still shivering even after they moved me closer to the fire. In the end they recommended that I sleep at one of their houses, at Hamadi Abu al-Issa's, and I agreed right away. He started up his Kia and brought me over to his place, where he lived with his sister and his mother, in a house around here, in this neighborhood. He woke up his sister to offer me her bed and a cup of coffee. After I was done drinking it, he said goodnight and left the room. But I felt as though I had already slept and eaten the food of the gods.

In the morning I woke up to find Abu Mahmoud was with me at Hamadi's, and the two of them were having coffee. I used the bathroom before joining them, said good morning, and they wished me an even better one, then we were served breakfast before Hamadi took us to the bus station so we could head back to Aleppo. Even more generous, he wouldn't let us pay our own fare, purchasing tickets for us.

I'm in that same area now... here at the al-Amasi restaurant. I turned off toward the right and found the building just to the left in front of me. I walked closer, knocked on the door, and his sister came out to greet me. When I asked her about him, she said, "He left for Turkey, he and his wife and children." When she asked what I wanted, I said, "Nothing..."

I drew away from her, cursing my rotten luck, and went back to where I was going to sleep, laid down on the bed, and began to review the day ahead of me.

By 8:30 I was dressed and had gone downstairs to meet Bahaa, also known as Abu Muhammad. He had only been waiting for me in the restaurant for a few minutes. He gracefully called over the waiter and ordered a kilo of mixed grilled meats, salad and vegetables, laban, hummus, and ayran to drink, and the man hurried away to put in our order.

The mujahid Abu Muhammad was armed to the teeth. There was a Russian rifle resting against the seat beside him, a pistol attached to his belt, and two grenades on his chest.

"We had such a good time together in Paris," I said.

"Those days are dead and gone," he said. "We live for today." He talked to me about jihad and how forbearance on the day of battle is deemed better by God than a hundred thousand days a believer spends in prayer and piety. "Those believers who fight against the enemies of God herald the coming of heaven, a heaven full of delight where people eat and drink by the grace of God."

"What do you do exactly?" I asked.

"Jihad in the path of God," he replied. "The most merciful and exalted God has revealed himself to me. After all those years in France, one day I went down into the street from your friend Abd al-Qadir's place to see the owner of a bookshop. I was looking for *The Collected Miracles of the Saints* by Sheikh Yusuf al-Nabhani. He asked me why I wanted it, and I told him it was to educate myself. At this point he left the bookstore to his daughter and walked with me, without leaving my side until I had become half a mujahid. The second time he showed me the way. The third time he handed me a plane ticket to Istanbul, where I was to meet Sheikh Abu al-Waleed al-Rihani in the airport, and then he would show me the straight path.

"I didn't come across any obstacles. As soon as I passed through security and passport control at the Istanbul airport and walked outside, I spotted him there, dressed in Pakistani clothes. He smiled when he first saw me, and I felt as though I were in the arms of my mother and father. He picked up my bag and we both hopped into a black four-wheel drive. Then we reached his home, or at least the place where we were all going to meet. He told me I must be tired and that I might like to rest until he could finish preparing some food for us. I washed up and performed my ablutions, and by the time I got back the food was ready. We expressed our thanks to God and ate. Then he invited me to go to sleep, and when I woke up we could have a nice chat. I surrendered myself to a pleasant slumber, as if my soul had never known comfort before.

"Anyway, my friend, the important thing is that I rested there. And the next day, after breakfast, he invited me to continue on to Diyarbekir. He had reserved a bus ticket for me, and from there onward to Tel Abyad, then to Raqqa, where I was to hand myself over to Sheikh Abu al-Khattab al-Anzi."

At this point, the waiter came over with appetizers and a bowl of laban and we started eating.

"My first job was to deliver my passport to the security office," Abu Muhammad went on to tell me, "then to complete a training course in all kinds of weapons, both light and heavy, and then to take a class on religion, in which I replenished my religious knowledge from the time I was a child, then a lesson in jihad, a course in Arabic language, and then the Arabic language teacher declared me proficient enough to teach Arabic myself."

Then another waiter came over with the grilled meat on a bed of rice covered with bread. Shaykh Abu Muhammad pulled the bread away, revealing the *mansaf* and chunks of grilled meat. How could anyone be this hungry, you might ask. They brought kebab and steak and lamb shanks and we tucked into the food. He stopped talking and I didn't say a word. The owner of the restaurant started paying attention to us, or to Abu Muhammad, really. He handed him a CD about jihad and fighting the enemy, about the heaven that awaited all the mujahideen.

Even after we had eaten our fill, there was still a lot of meat left over, so he started goading me into eating more, encouraging me to have some without the bread. I told him I had had enough, thank God for this bounty.

"Eat something, man," he told me. "You haven't finished a thing."

He was force-feeding me, scraping hunks of meat onto my plate, until I said, "That's enough, honestly."

He asked the waiter to bring us something from the sweets shop next door, and he brought us a kilo of *kanafeh* pastry.

"Shame on you, your body can't take all of this."

He laughed, saying, "Don't you worry about it. We can do whatever we want."

As I nibbled on one piece of dessert, Abu Muhammad asked the waiter to wrap up everything that was left over so he could take it with him. The waiter tidied up the table, placing all the leftovers into a bag. After finishing our tea we stood up. I tried to pay the bill but the owner refused to take my money, telling me, "Your money's no good here, just give the waiter five hundred liras."

The waiter carried the doggie bag out to the Mercedes for us. Abu Muhammad and I sat down in the car and took off. We headed north and then west. He told me he was going to pass by the house so he could put the food there. His house was right near the mayor's mansion, in an expensive, brand-new building, on a street they call Villa Row. He didn't take me inside with him, and when he came back after a bit I asked him to take me somewhere I could rest and then come pick me up later to take me to the market. I walked into the hotel, waving goodbye to him in more or less the same way I had said hello a little while earlier.

Early the next morning I went over to Abu Muhammad's place on Villa Row and rang the bell but nobody answered. I waited for some time, until a member of the Islamic State came to greet me. When I asked about him, the man demanded, "Who is he to you?"

"He's a friend," I said, "I've known him a long time."

"He's gone off on a jihad operation," he told me.

"Where?"

"I can't tell you that."

"But he's a good friend of mine."

He simply repeated that he had departed on a jihad operation and that heaven was his final destination. I walked back to the hotel, packed up my things, and decided to return to Aleppo. I made my way back to the bus station, booked a seat, and then boarded the bus, waiting for it to depart.

The bus was all set to leave the garage when a bearded man whose hair had grown out long hopped on board. He was dressed in the uniform of the Islamic State, bristling with guns and grenades. He scrutinized the face of each and every one of us, studying us carefully, then proceeded to the women in the back of the bus and started chatting with one of them. There were eight women back there, all sitting primly in their seats, all had draped their niqabs down to cover their faces. They were dressed in black from head to toe. When the man came back toward the front of the bus, I asked him what he wanted with that one woman in particular.

"Brother, everybody knows how women are supposed to dress in the Islamic State, everyone except for this one apparently."

"What about her?" I asked.

"She sasses me and says she's been dressing this way her entire life. She deserves to be whipped."

"Forgive her, sheikh."

"May God protect us from them," he muttered as he walked away.

The young woman was wearing dark purple, and he insisted that she should be dressed exclusively in black.

I looked out the window at the street below as the bus sped off. There was a child with ISIS walking around the garage, a little kid who couldn't have been more than ten years old carrying a Russian-made rifle, dressed in camouflage like all the other Islamic State fighters. As soon as the bus started to veer off toward the right, I felt as though I were saying farewell to the river as we crossed over it in that moment. I shut my eyes and surrendered to oblivion for a moment. What was I going to tell my wife? Should I tell her I wasn't able to find Hamadi Abu al-Issa? Or that I couldn't find a house to rent? I think I'll tell her what happened to me, and maybe I'll come back soon. The taste of the Euphrates water was still on my tongue.

In the past I used to travel to Raqqa and from there on to Damascus. Along the Raqqa highway you would pass through Al-Sukhnah and Palmyra. The road to Aleppo was blocked off. There was only one way to cross over there and that was the Raqqa highway. I had reserved myself a seat on a bus that would first go to Damascus. We didn't pass too much on the way down there. I stared out the window at the sky, gloomy and dark, not overcast because of clouds but thick with black smoke. The smell inside the bus was intense.

"They're extracting oil and barreling it," said a man on the bus.

I could have sworn I saw specters of men covered in black directing a primitive refining operation. There were black dots all over the place, human beings extracting petroleum coated in black, their clothes and their bodies alike. Everyone was hard at work. They were transporting the crude oil in containers for sale at the marketplace. They loaded it into barrels, sold it as diesel and gasoline. The market was located just before you reach Tabqa. There were cars waiting to deliver the barrels to areas not under regime control.

As soon as we had made it to areas that didn't reek of petroleum, we were stopped at a checkpoint. Someone from the Islamic State boarded the bus and said, *"As-salaamu aleikum,"* some of us replied to him, others said nothing at all. He began by giving us a sermon about the significance of the pious cloak, how the Prophet had sent one to the Ruler of Egypt, al-Muqawqis, telling us that entire story before going on to tell us how deeply he came to believe in Islam when he heard the tale of the cloak. He was addressing us in modern standard Arabic, telling us how he used to be a law student but then left that behind to join up with the Islamic State. He told us all to extend our hands as he pulled out a small nail clipper and began cutting fingernails, not everyone's, of course, just those with long ones, insisting that all hands should look like women's. When he had made it all the way to the back of the bus he began to walk forward again, chitchatting with the bus attendant, and he concluded by threatening to skin him alive if he ever saw passengers with such long fingernails again. He disembarked from the bus, wishing us all a pleasant journey.

"God is good," the bus driver told us, then invited the women among us to dress however they felt like and said that none of us would say a word.

I turned to his assistant and asked, "What's the matter with you, man? You just let him cut our fingernails like that. Do you have glue in your mouth or something, brother?"

And we set off once again.

The bus continued all the way to Tabqa, where we turned off to the left. The airport was on one side. It appeared totally abandoned. After a while I saw more oil extraction taking place, something like thirty-three derricks, all of them seemed to be brand new, some were active, others were not. There were pipelines to transport the oil. You would have seen a highly coordinated operation that begins with extraction and refining here, then transport somewhere else, only God and the Islamic State know where exactly.

The bus attendant had gone to bring the women water several times. When we were out of ISIS territory, he returned to the back of the bus to take the flyers the man had given them in the garage. I took one from him and read a piece of paper addressing "My Muslim Sister," imploring her to respect the law of God, to wear the niqab and to always wear the same bulky gown that was worn by the Prophet's wives. I turned around to look at them. The women were all bustling to tear off the veils from their faces and the outer gowns from their bodies. Suddenly they were all wearing jeans and blouses, some of them already with makeup, while others applied cosmetics to their faces, all except for that one woman whom the guy from ISIS had threatened to whip when she told him that she had dressed like this her entire life.

The bus attendant tore up the papers and tossed the scraps out the window. We continued through the seemingly endless countryside for an hour and a half. The youngsters pulled out their mobile phones and started playing games,

while the women returned to their seats beside their husbands, at least until we reached the first regime checkpoint.
We passed through five checkpoints in total before arriving at
Athriya, the crossing point for those coming from Salamiyah,
Damascus and Beirut, Tartous, Latakia, Hama, the villages
of Idlib and their hinterlands, and those going onward to
al-Shaar and Bustan al-Qasr. I don't think these people
were from around here. I thought they were from Aleppo,
and their only way out was through Al-Safira, that's what I
thought anyway.

We reached Khanasir, then Al-Safira. There were villages
scattered here and there completely devoid of people. All the
doors and windows had been thrown open, soldiers loyal to
the regime were sitting on refrigerators and washing machines
all over the place. The regime army was the sole military force
present. Birds congregating in the road flew away when the
buses rumbled past, squawking at us.

As we crossed the Al-Safira road we started to notice people who weren't dressed in military fatigues. At the checkpoints
where we were stopped, we paid a bribe along with a bottle of
fresh water, until the bus reached the Ramouseh checkpoint.
By this point the bus attendant had collected all of our identification documents so the information could be entered into
the computer for a security check. We waited about half an
hour before we were finally cleared to enter Aleppo.

ROUNDABOUT OF DEATH

The next day I went back to the Island Cafe, where the young men had gathered around the table without me on that dark night with no crescent moon. As soon as I sat down at the table, they said in unison: "Welcome back." How could all this be happening when I hadn't told anyone anything about what I had been up to in the first place? Before walking inside I anxiously searched the mirror for any lumps of arousal poking through my hair.

Muhammad D wasn't there yet, but I learned that his brother had been shot in the right foot by a sniper and was now in the hospital. When Muhammad D showed up two hours later and sat down right next to me, I asked him how the situation was now, and he said his brother had been taken for surgery at the Razi Hospital, that he'd have to stay there for a few days to undergo a second operation.

"Where did the bullet that struck him come from?" I asked.

He carefully looked around, remained silent, then looked back in our direction. "I think . . . " he said, looking around again, and even though there wasn't anyone there, he whispered in my ear. "It was the regime, my brother's with them, but they wanted to teach him a lesson, he had been dragging his feet, never really cared about them, it was a warning shot, a message to him, they don't even know about his illness. Behind the toaster oven there was a curtain that was supposed to protect against snipers, the poor guy couldn't imagine they'd ever be able to shoot him, and as soon as he placed his leg in the building exit they opened fire, his heel shattered into bits, and they're going to have to order a plate to put in his foot."

"It's all in God's hands now," I said.

"Is there anything worse than a sniper?" Muhammad D asked. "Muhammad B, that's right, he's the pilot who dropped barrel bombs on the old city of Aleppo, he's sure there were no fighters there from Jabhat al-Nusra or the Free Syrian Army, and still he dropped barrels that killed people and flattened their homes. Now they're even starting to use water mines, so our sea is secure but we aren't safe inside."

"Guys," I said, "change the subject already, let's talk about women instead."

No electricity, no water, no gas in the house, and we just got news about my son Nawwar. His mother relayed it to me, that he had arrived safely in Istanbul and found work there, you can all relax, I hope you're all fine, he wrote.

"Thank God for everything," I said, "and curse all the evil things in the world."

I went over to see my mother, and she said, "C'mon, let's

go see your sister Shukriya, to offer condolences about her two boys."

"What's going on with her?" I asked. "Which two boys?" as if I didn't understand a thing. As we headed toward her house my mother explained everything, how her two boys had been killed, one who was with the regime and the other one who was with the opposition, and she was holding the mourning ceremony for them in the street outside her home.

We arrived at her house to find people seated there for the mourning ceremony. A bunch of young men dressed in camouflage showed up, all of them sons of my powerful sister, and at this point the reader at the ceremony began to recite from the Quran.

I took advantage of the opportunity to pop inside my sister Shukriya's house. When I kissed her on the cheek and encouraged her to take comfort in religion and her faith, she muttered something incomprehensible in response. I kissed my other sister and sat down next to my two siblings, my mother across from me, women and children surrounding me. We're all together on this road, I said. One sister gave me prayer beads and she gave my mother some beads, too. We sat there for a little while, then said our goodbyes and left.

Now here I sit in the cafe all alone. There's nobody else left at the table. As I think about everything that has happened, I muse to myself: Tomorrow's only a day away. I waited for an hour, two hours, and when nobody came, I stood up and went to buy some vegetables. I took a shared taxi to the new part of Aleppo, the southern part, the roundabout of death.

FAYSAL KHARTASH is a leading Syrian author. He lives in his native Aleppo, has written several novels and works as a school teacher while contributing to Syrian newspapers.

MAX WEISS teaches the history of the modern Middle East at Princeton University. He has translated books by Nihad Sirees, Dunya Mikhail and Samar Yazbek.

THE DRIVE
BY YAIR ASSULIN

This mesmerizing novel tells the journey of a young Israeli soldier at the breaking point, unable to continue carrying out his military service, yet terrified of the consequences of leaving the army. As the soldier and his father embark on a lengthy drive to meet with a military psychiatrist, Yair Assulin penetrates the torn world of the hero, whose journey is not just that of a young man facing a crucial dilemma, but a tour of the soul and depths of Israeli society and of those everywhere who resist regimentation and violence.

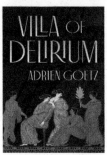

VILLA OF DELIRIUM
BY ADRIEN GOETZ

Along the French Riviera, an illustrious family in thrall to classical antiquity builds a fabulous villa—a replica of a Greek palace, complete with marble columns, furniture of exotic wwoods and frescoes depicting mythological gods. The Reinachs—related to other wealthy Jews like the Rothschilds and the Ephrussis—attempt in the early 1900s to recreate "a pure beauty" lost to modernity and fill it with the pursuit of pleasure and knowledge. This is a Greek epic for the modern era.

AND THE BRIDE CLOSED THE DOOR
BY RONIT MATALON

A young bride shuts herself up in a bedroom on her wedding day, refusing to get married. In this moving and humorous look at contemporary Israel and the chaotic ups and downs of love everywhere, her family gathers outside the locked door, not knowing what to do. The only communication they receive from behind the door are scribbled notes, one of them a cryptic poem about a prodigal daughter returning home. The harder they try to reach the defiant woman, the more the despairing groom is convinced that her refusal should be respected. But what, exactly, ought to be respected? Is this merely a case of cold feet?

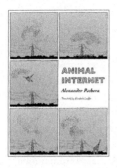

ANIMAL INTERNET
BY ALEXANDER PSCHERA

Some 50,000 creatures around the globe—
including whales, leopards, flamingoes, bats and
snails—are being equipped with digital tracking
devices. The data gathered and studied by major
scientific institutes about their behavior will warn
us about tsunamis, earthquakes and volcanic
eruptions, but also radically transform our
relationship to the natural world. Contrary to
pessimistic fears, author Alexander Pschera sees the Internet as creating a
historic opportunity for a new dialogue between man and nature.

EXPOSED
BY JEAN-PHILIPPE BLONDEL

A dangerous intimacy emerges between a French
teacher and a former student who has achieved
art world celebrity. The painting of a portrait
upturns both their lives. Jean-Philippe Blondel,
author of the bestselling novel *The 6:41 to Paris,*
evokes an intimacy of dangerous intensity in a
stunning tale about aging, regret and moving
ahead into the future.

THE 6:41 TO PARIS
BY JEAN-PHILIPPE BLONDEL

Cécile, a stylish 47-year-old, has spent the
weekend visiting her parents outside Paris. By
Monday morning, she's exhausted. These trips
back home are stressful and she settles into a train
compartment with an empty seat beside her. But
it's soon occupied by a man she recognizes as
Philippe Leduc, with whom she had a passionate
affair that ended in her brutal humiliation 30
years ago. In the fraught hour and a half that ensues, Cécile and Philippe
hurtle towards the French capital in a psychological thriller about the pain
and promise of past romance.

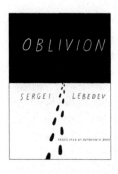

OBLIVION
BY SERGEI LEBEDEV

In one of the first 21st century Russian novels to probe the legacy of the Soviet prison camp system, a young man travels to the vast wastelands of the Far North to uncover the truth about a shadowy neighbor who saved his life, and whom he knows only as Grandfather II. Emerging from today's Russia, where the ills of the past are being forcefully erased from public memory, this masterful novel represents an epic literary attempt to rescue history from the brink of oblivion.

THE YEAR OF THE COMET
BY SERGEI LEBEDEV

A story of a Russian boyhood and coming of age as the Soviet Union is on the brink of collapse. Lebedev depicts a vast empire coming apart at the seams, transforming a very public moment into something tender and personal, and writes with stunning beauty and shattering insight about childhood and the growing consciousness of a boy in the world.

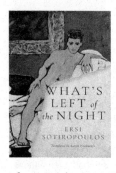

WHAT'S LEFT OF THE NIGHT
BY ERSI SOTIROPOULOS

Constantine Cavafy arrives in Paris in 1897 on a trip that will deeply shape his future and push him toward his poetic inclination. With this lyrical novel, tinged with an hallucinatory eroticism that unfolds over three unforgettable days, celebrated Greek author Ersi Sotiropoulos depicts Cavafy in the midst of a journey of self-discovery across a continent on the brink of massive change. A stunning portrait of a budding author—before he became C.P. Cavafy, one of the 20th century's greatest poets—that illuminates the complex relationship of art, life, and the erotic desires that trigger creativity.

THE EYE
BY PHILIPPE COSTAMAGNA

It's a rare and secret profession, comprising a few dozen people around the world equipped with a mysterious mixture of knowledge and innate sensibility. Summoned to Swiss bank vaults, Fifth Avenue apartments, and Tokyo storerooms, they are entrusted by collectors, dealers, and museums to decide if a coveted picture is real or fake and to determine if it was painted by Leonardo da Vinci or Raphael. *The Eye* lifts the veil on the rarified world of connoisseurs devoted to the authentication and discovery of Old Master artworks.

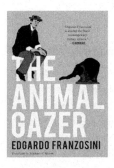

THE ANIMAL GAZER
BY EDGARDO FRANZOSINI

A hypnotic novel inspired by the strange and fascinating life of sculptor Rembrandt Bugatti, brother of the fabled automaker. Bugatti obsessively observes and sculpts the baboons, giraffes, and panthers in European zoos, finding empathy with their plight and identifying with their life in captivity. Rembrandt Bugatti's work, now being rediscovered, is displayed in major art museums around the world and routinely fetches large sums at auction. Edgardo Franzosini recreates the young artist's life with intense lyricism, passion, and sensitivity.

ALLMEN AND THE DRAGONFLIES
BY MARTIN SUTER

Johann Friedrich von Allmen has exhausted his family fortune by living in Old World grandeur despite present-day financial constraints. Forced to downscale, Allmen inhabits the garden house of his former Zurich estate, attended by his Guatemalan butler, Carlos. This is the first of a series of humorous, fast-paced detective novels devoted to a memorable gentleman thief. A thrilling art heist escapade infused with European high culture and luxury that doesn't shy away from the darker side of human nature.

THE MADELEINE PROJECT
BY CLARA BEAUDOUX

A young woman moves into a Paris apartment and discovers a storage room filled with the belongings of the previous owner, a certain Madeleine who died in her late nineties, and whose treasured possessions nobody seems to want. In an audacious act of journalism driven by personal curiosity and humane tenderness, Clara Beaudoux embarks on *The Madeleine Project*, documenting what she finds on Twitter with text and photographs, introducing the world to an unsung 20th century figure.

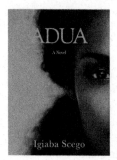

ADUA
BY IGIABA SCEGO

Adua, an immigrant from Somalia to Italy, has lived in Rome for nearly forty years. She came seeking freedom from a strict father and an oppressive regime, but her dreams of film stardom ended in shame. Now that the civil war in Somalia is over, her homeland calls her. She must decide whether to return and reclaim her inheritance, but also how to take charge of her own story and build a future.

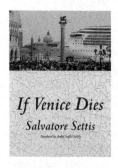

IF VENICE DIES
BY SALVATORE SETTIS

Internationally renowned art historian Salvatore Settis ignites a new debate about the Pearl of the Adriatic and cultural patrimony at large. In this fiery blend of history and cultural analysis, Settis argues that "hit-and-run" visitors are turning Venice and other landmark urban settings into shopping malls and theme parks. This is a passionate plea to secure the soul of Venice, written with consummate authority, wide-ranging erudition and élan.

I BELONG TO VIENNA
BY ANNA GOLDENBERG

In autumn 1942, Anna Goldenberg's great-grandparents and one of their sons are deported to the Theresienstadt concentration camp. Hans, their elder son, survives by hiding in an apartment in the middle of Nazi-controlled Vienna. Goldenberg reconstructs this unique story in magnificent reportage. A probing tale of heroism, resilience, identity and belonging, marked by a surprising freshness as a new generation comes to terms with history's darkest era.

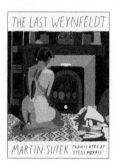

THE LAST WEYNFELDT
BY MARTIN SUTER

Adrian Weynfeldt is an art expert in an international auction house, a bachelor in his mid-fifties living in a grand Zurich apartment filled with costly paintings and antiques. Always correct and well-mannered, he's given up on love until one night—entirely out of character for him—Weynfeldt decides to take home a ravishing but unaccountable young woman and gets embroiled in an art forgery scheme that threatens his buttoned up existence. This refined page-turner moves behind elegant bourgeois facades into darker recesses of the heart.

MOVING THE PALACE
BY CHARIF MAJDALANI

A young Lebanese adventurer explores the wilds of Africa, encountering an eccentric English colonel in Sudan and enlisting in his service. In this lush chronicle of far-flung adventure, the military recruit crosses paths with a compatriot who has dismantled a sumptuous palace and is transporting it across the continent on a camel caravan. This is a captivating modern-day Odyssey in the tradition of Bruce Chatwin and Paul Theroux.

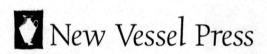

New Vessel Press

To purchase these titles and for more information
please visit newvesselpress.com.